I0625898

Legends of Carpatia

Melania Tolan

Copyright © 2016 by **Melania Tolan**

All rights reserved. No part of this publication may be reproduced, distributed or transmitted in any form or by any means, without prior written permission.

Melania Tolan
PO BOX 16222
PORTLAND, OR 97216
www.melania.tolan.blogspot.com

Publisher's Note: The author acknowledges the copyrighted or trademarked status and the trademark owners of any workmarks mentioned in the work of fiction.

Cover Design by Victoria Cooper Art

Yule's Eve/ Melania Tolan. -- 1st ed.
ISBN 978-0-9904007-8-3

Yule's Eve

A Legends of Carpatia Tale

This book is dedicated to Tanti Luci.

The ancient vampire quivered as he passed through the strong wards set by the gypsy crone. He'd never understood their magic, but after thousands of years of roaming this earth, and witnessing events beyond anyone's wildest imagination, he knew anything could be possible. He didn't question why this particular witch could set up magic barriers so strong that the oldest vampire couldn't break, yet he could waltz right in. He knew his hefty gold payment had nothing to do with this either, as there were far more wealthy immortals around who could easily surpass his compensation by a hundred-fold. Yet here he was again.

"You may enter, Traian." Her voice came from the small hut hidden deep in the woods at the foothills of the Carpathian Mountains.

Gypsies rarely wandered alone this far from their clans, but she wasn't just any old gypsy. Satra preferred the solitude of the forest to the chaotic cacophony of the camp where her people lived. This worked out perfectly for him. No one needed to know about his dealings with her.

He came to the door of the hut and paused, needing to prepare his mind for what he was about to experience. Traian pushed open the door, entered the one-room structure, and tried not to cringe. Everything about gypsy magic was meant to repel the undead, and Satra had made no exception for him.

Smoke and the smells of items hanging from her low ceiling filled his senses. The magic in the room thickened as he made his way to the center of the hut. He shouldn't have come, but here he stood, in the middle of a century-old gypsy witch's home. Just as he'd had for years. Yule's Eve was one of the most powerful nights of the year for magic, and she would help him harness some of that energy.

At the center of the room, hunched over a steaming cauldron, stood Satra. At her age, she shouldn't be living alone so far away from her people, but Traian knew that as frail and weathered as she appeared, she could cast spells strong enough to bind him into the underworld for centuries with only a snap of her arthritic fingers. One could argue that she might be one of the vampires' worst enemies, yet he never feared her. Respect, yes, but never fear. She'd been the only one to understand his secret.

"Good evening, Satra," he greeted her in a hushed tone as if he were in a sanctuary, not that he ever attended church.

Christian magic prevented all undead from stepping upon their sacred ground.

"Your sacrifice." She held out a knife.

He took the blade, slicing a long line along his left palm and quickly squeezing five drops into the cauldron, before his skin healed moments later.

"Lie down." She waved toward the lounge covered in faded tapestries and blankets next to the fire. Satra never cared for small talk. That's why he liked her.

He did as she'd asked and rested his head against the back of the chaise. Within moments she stood by his side with a steaming cup of potion. Her magic always did a number on him. He would pay dearly for the next twenty-four hours after drinking this, but the prize was well worth the physical cost. Without hesitation, he took the cup and drank the potion in one gulp. The hot fluid scalded the back of his throat, but he didn't care; the tissue would heal soon enough. When the potion reached his stomach, he lurched forward, bracing his waist with both hands. The ceramic cup hit the packed dirt floor and broke into three pieces.

No matter how much he prepared himself for this, the initial pain always caught him off guard. His body convulsed as his conscious state clouded. He felt as if he were traveling through time — which in a way he was — as his subconscious took over. "Yule. Take me to Yule's Eve," he whispered before losing all motor control. Traian's mind and the magic of the potion obeyed. One last convulsion and he lay still, eyes open as if seeing something that had happened long ago, back when his heart still beat.

***

Traian found himself in the middle of the snowy East woods, carrying a pole on which were fastened the fruits of his labor. The celebration of Winter Solstice meant everyone in the village contributed to the festival. Even children helped by collecting pinecones and boughs of fir to decorate the hall. Craftsmen built chairs and tables for everyone to have a place to sit, and the tanners made pelts to cover the couches around the fire. Cooks prepared a variety of different roasts, porridges and soups. Platters of breads, cakes, and pastries were presented by the bakers themselves. Talented seamstresses had fashioned gowns so fancy they were fit for rulers. Even the healers busied themselves preparing elixirs to help with over-stuffed bellies.

Everyone had a job, including the village hunter. Early

this morning Traian had gone out and now his pole held a fat doe and four rabbits. Their weight slowed his steps and made walking back to the village through the knee-deep snow difficult. He leaned against a tree to rest when he heard a crackling, buzzing sound nearby. Traian sucked the winter air into his lungs and straightened his back. He would not be caught slouching on the job, especially by *her*. Who knew what kinds of hexes she might unleash upon him. Traian released his breath and inhaled again, deeply. There it was. Her scent. Fir, lavender, and rosemary. He turned his head to the right and peered around the tree.

Evelina stood with her back to him. He watched in awe, forgetting for a moment the weight on his shoulders. He'd seen her at work before when he'd first moved to the village in late summer, but he had always kept his distance. He didn't trust magic. Something that couldn't be explained should be feared, or at least avoided. Though he'd seen other magicians in his young lifetime, he'd never witnessed anything like the power this young woman could produce. Where did she get it?

He watched her weave a web of fire and light from tree to tree, while murmuring an incantation to herself. Her golden curls fluttered away from her face as she worked, and she moved closer to his position until she was almost a stone's throw away. When she turned her head and looked directly into his eyes, Evelina asked, "Were you going to greet me or just stand there like a knot on a log?"

Traian nearly dropped his game to the ground. "My apologies. I meant no intrusion. I shall be going now." He hoisted his load securely onto his shoulders, shook the loose strands of hair from his eyes, and took steps to walk away from the magic fence she had created.

"Why do you always avoid me?"

He stopped, but did not turn to face her.

"I've seen you in the village since summer," she continued. "You always change your course when you see me coming. Apparently, you never like to be in the same building with me. The one time we came face to face at the village market, you merely said hello and ran away. Are you afraid of me?"

Emotions flooded Traian's mind and heart. Afraid, yes. She scared him to his marrow. He didn't like things he couldn't explain, especially when they looked the way she did, tantalizingly luscious. The curves of her body begged to be touched and explored. The tops of her plump breasts, threatening to slip forth from the flattering dresses she wore, stirred something inside his groin that hadn't been awakened in a long time. When she smiled, all the blood drained below his waist. Someone with that kind of power over him should be feared, never mind the actual magic powers she wielded. He'd take a bear or a saber tooth tiger bare-handed any day over this sort of temptation.

"I am not evil," she said, "if it's that which worries you."

"I never thought you were." Traian hurried away before he fell under her spell.

***

The effects of the crone's magic continued to course through Traian's body, and abruptly the scene changed. He now stood at the center of the village. He adjusted the leather coat over his tunic, and smoothed black hair back into the cord that held the locks at the base of his neck. The sound of festivities met his ears long before he spotted the great hall. As he made his way through the snow towards the building, the smells of the festival met his nose and his stomach growled in response. Nothing prepared him for the merrymaking inside. Traian opened the great, white wood door and entered an enchanted winter land.

Boughs of fir and spruce laced with red, purple, blue, and silver ribbons wrapped around the high rafters, creating a canopy of greenery as if they were in the middle of a forest. Candles and torches lit the room with warm, inviting light. The tables lining the outer walls overflowed with platters filled with every kind of food imaginable and available in the winter. Potatoes, pickled vegetables, meats, cheeses, breads, and roasts. Then there was the dessert table. Never in all of Traian's years had he seen so many different sweet treats. Towards the back of the hall, a group of musicians played jolly music that had inspired half of the village to dance around the hall, while others chose to sit and fill their bellies with delights from the tables.

A massive fire burned brightly from the center of the room and that's where he spotted her. His breath caught in his throat as he feasted on the magnificent beauty before him. She stood like a goddess, light from the fire catching the silver threads of her white dress, a red cape thrown over her shoulders giving her an otherworldly glow. He'd seen her many times since his arrival in the village. He'd spied on her in the woods while hunting and watched her weave her earth magic, seen her tend to the sick in the village by healing a variety of ailments, and observed her working with the village leaders. She may even be the reason he stood in this hall tonight. Among all the settlements in Carpatia, they were the only village to avoid attack from the barbarian tribes of the north, or the brutes from the south, probably because no one knew of their existence. They were hidden well in this valley, but he knew it was only a matter of time before they would be discovered.

His own village had already been burned and decimated by the Southern Savages. Traian had returned from a hunt at dawn, met by the smell of seared flesh and ashes. Nothing was left but the smoldering remnants of the prosperous community that had once thrived there. With nowhere to go, he'd fled to the mountains and lived off the land, but as winter approached, he knew he needed to find a more permanent shelter. By sheer fortuity he stumbled upon this sheltered valley of the great Carpathian Mountains while stalking a large buck. He soon discovered the village and the sorceress who protected its people from evils both seen and unseen.

Traian didn't need her protection, but curiosity kept him here, at least until spring. He was a simple man with simple needs. Magic and myth had no place in his life. Yet here he stood, watching the ethereal sorceress entertain the children at the center of the room. They openly accepted her "gifts." He hadn't reached that point yet.

With the children's rapt attention, she made the fire turn purple, then green, then blue. They squealed in delight at the colors, gasping as she reached into the flames and brought out a ball of fire in her palms. His own breath caught in his chest at the sight, but her delicate hands never changed color or shape, nor did he smell burning human flesh. She whispered to the flame and higher it danced, tongues of fire twirling to her bidding until they formed a star. The fiery star broke from the main source in her hands and floated up over the fire pit. Cheers and laughter broke out over the small crowd that had gathered around the children.

She continued to make shapes of animals and creatures, some of which he'd never seen before. A dragon got the biggest applause as it flew over the crowd and around the room several times before burning out. Her magic was indeed formidable, but he still had doubts. These people believed in things that did not exist. He'd heard of dragons, but in his village, they were only tales told to children to keep them from wandering into the woods alone. Bears, lions, and wolves…these were threats they faced, not dragons.

Traian forced himself away from the spectacle to find sustenance to fill his belly. Once at the tables of food, he filled a wooden plate with goat cheese and pieces of the roasted game he'd caught earlier. Flavors danced in his mouth as he devoured each morsel. When he finished with the savory options he moved on to the sweets. Never in his life had he tasted anything more delicious than the winter spice cake that was unique to this village.

"It's good, isn't it?" An equally delicious voice came from behind him, sending a flurry of butterflies from his chest down to his feet, making the hair covering his arms stand at attention. "I think I already had five of those today."

He nearly choked on the last piece he'd stuffed in his mouth. "You? Where would you fit them in your small frame?" He ignored the tension forming between his shoulders.

She tilted her head back and let out a hearty laugh that warmed every cold corner of his body. "I put away more food than you can catch, my dear Hunter."

He turned to her. "Can you now? Let's see." To his surprise, he welcomed the playful banter. Her magic might be terrifying, but the levity of her spirit refreshed his soul.

She smirked at him and grabbed a platter. "Challenge accepted." Before he could blink twice, she'd filled a wooden plate with spice cake, fruit cake, and other sweets from the table. He watched her move to the cheeses and fill every little space that was left. "Come, let's sit."

Cautiously, he followed her to an empty spot by the fire. She sat down gracefully despite the heavy-laden platter in her hands. There wasn't much space beside her, but she tilted her head for him to sit next to her. The nearer he got, the tighter his nerves pulled. This was the closest he'd ever been to a sorceress. He could feel magic crackling around her and it set his alarms off. Was this a trap? Had she cast a spell on him?

Listen to yourself. Just because you've seen a few festival tricks doesn't mean magic is real. But he'd seen so much since he'd taken residence in the village. He pushed his concerns away and sat next to her. "You really plan on eating all of that?"

"Of course." She'd already begun. "Fire manipulation takes energy. Magic isn't free, you know. There's always a price to pay."

"Right." He nodded.

"You're still a skeptic...after all you've seen?"

He shrugged.

"Why?"

"I only believe in what can be explained, and eyes can be deceived."

"Oh dear." She chuckled, "You will discover many things can't be explained in our mortal tongues."

This touched upon one of his deepest fears. The longer he lived in Carpatia, the stranger the sightings and events he'd witnessed. Most of them were linked to her, but not all. Once he'd seen a winged child zipping through the forest from tree to tree like a hummingbird. She disappeared as quickly as she had appeared. But the strangest, however, had happened this morning when he watched Evelina weave a fence of invisible fire around the village in preparation for the festival. That had scared him witless and he almost hadn't come tonight for fear he would run into her. Now here he sat next to the most powerful creature he'd ever encountered.

"Why do you still fear me?" she asked between mouthfuls of food.

He stifled a shudder. Had she read his mind? He considered retreating to his burdei on the outskirts of the village. Instead, he sat there, rubbing his sweaty palms together. The conflict of wanting to be close to her... but also wanting to get away from her… waged in his belly. "I do not know." He spoke the truth. He truly didn't know, but he wanted to find out why.

"Hmm." She mulled and popped another spice cake into her mouth. When she finished, she set the nearly empty platter on the small wooden stool next to her. "Come, I need to show you something."

She stood and held out her hand. Reluctantly, he took it. She led him through the crowd to the back of the hall and out the side door. They slipped into the snowy night and wandered through the village until they reached the forest. His shoulders tensed more as they continued into the darkened East woods, closer to the invisible fence he'd seen her weave earlier.

They reached the boundary, and with a wave of her free hand, a section of the magic barrier appeared and an opening formed. She tightened her grip on his hand as she pulled him through the portal. Sparks of magic danced across his skin as he passed through. He glanced over his shoulder and watched as the opening shut and the fence disappeared, his exit now closed. This should have unnerved him, but for some reason he felt excited, not afraid. He should be wary of being alone in the woods with her, but he wasn't. The lusty sensations tingling in his groin blurred his logic, putting him in a potentially dangerous position.

Deeper into the forest they walked until they began climbing the side of one of the mountains surrounding the village. A red flame in her palm lit their way, casting shadows around them. He had not seen how she'd started the fire. It just appeared out of nowhere, like many things around her. Higher they climbed, until they reached a small opening in a rock, hidden in plain sight by overgrown shrubs and layers of snow.

Evelina whispered and a portal formed in the middle of the snow and branches, similar the one that opened in the invisible fence. Tightening her grip again, she pulled him into a cave he hadn't known existed. In the last few months, he had combed these mountains while hunting and gathering with the village residents. On each outing, he'd created a mental map of the area should the same demise fall upon these people that had his own. He knew it was only a matter of time before the Southern Savages would come and pillage this settlement.

The tight tunnel through the rock twisted and turned. Many other channels branched off on both sides, creating a labyrinth of passageways. The flame in Evelina's palm cast an eerie light on the jagged walls. One could easily become lost in here if they didn't know their way. After a couple of turns, a small tunnel opened into a dark, vast space. Evelina released his hand, and immediately he missed the closeness, which surprised him. She took the flame in her hand, held it to the cave wall, and whispered a few inaudible words. A series of torches lit up around the wall of a cave with the same red flame. The cavern was so huge the entire village and gardens could fit comfortably inside.

Traian scanned the large room. Small coves peppered the periphery of the cave, all lit with red sconces. One cove had shelves full of jars, each a different color; another had various stones and crystals, but the one that caught his eye had a tapestry drawn across the entrance as a curtain. He wondered what secrets lay hidden behind the illuminated cloth.

The temperature inside the cavern seemed warm and inviting, like that of a burdei with a blazing fire in the hearth. Traian waved his hand over the nearest sconce and felt nothing. "It won't burn you." Evelina responded to his unasked question. He stuck his fingers in the flame long enough that he should smell singed skin. She was right. To the touch, the red fire was similar to a cool mist. He wondered what heat source warmed this vast cave.

"What is this place?" Traian turned away from the wall and gazed upward. The cave went on as if no roof existed.

Evelina smiled and spread her arms wide. "Welcome to my secret lair."

"Secret, eh? How secret can it be when you bring a stranger here?"

"You, my dear Hunter, are not a stranger." She paused. "Do you ever wonder why you were drawn here to this village?" she asked, pacing slowly around him.

He felt uneasy. Many threads of reason could fill the answer and they rattled in his bones. He replied to her question with a brief nod.

"I saw you. I saw your village." She took a deep breath in. "And its end."

"You saw *my* village?" His hands balled into fists, heat rising in his gut.

She held her hand out as if to calm his sudden flare of temper. "I was too late, for which I will never forgive myself. I should have listened to her, and now you suffer because of my lapse in judgment."

"You were there?"

"Right after the savages had left. I could have pursued them, but I couldn't take on their army alone, unprepared. I'd heard talk of those raids, but this was the first I'd seen with my own eyes. While I was busy caring for my people, our neighbors were being slaughtered, and there is no excuse for that." She stared into the distance, as if looking into another moment in time. Sadness clouded her moss-green eyes like a dark, grey storm.

"Why bring me here, and tell me this then?" The fire inside his bones subsided a notch.

Her focus shifted back to him. "Because you are our hope." She glanced over her shoulder to the center of the room. "At least according to her."

Her? He followed her gaze to a mound at the middle of the cavern. His eyes had adjusted to the light inside the room, and he noted tall spikes. As Traian studied their pattern he realized they were moving. The whole mound stirred and changed form, as if growing taller. Warm air shifted through the room from a gentle breeze to a hiss that grew louder by the second. Loose strands of his hair fluttered away from his face when a hot gust pushed him back a step. Instinct took over and he had his hunting knife out in a flash, just as he came face to face with a crimson head with orbs of fire for eyes. Its nostrils glowed in the low light.

"Hello, Hunter." The voice rumbled and hissed through every bone in his body. "At last we meet."

Traian didn't know whether to attack or run for dear life. Instead, he stood frozen in place.

"Easy, Hunter. She won't hurt you." Evelina held her hand up. He sensed the magic pouring from her palm, steadying his arms and feet, holding him still.

"Release me, witch." His fear dissipated and anger rose once more.

"That is no way to talk to my companion." The words came out in a hiss.

Evelina stepped between him and the creature. "I will release you, but only if you promise not to run or hurt her."

"I will slice your throat, demon." He growled back at the abomination and struggled against invisible bindings. The harder he tried to break free, the tighter the magic wrapped around his wrists and ankles.

"Traian, please. Be calm. We mean no harm."

"If that is true, then you must release me."

"Do you promise to listen, without violence?"

The magic tightened around his chest. He could barely breathe. "Release me." Traian gasped as black spots sprinkled his vision. He tried to maintain an iron grip on his knife, but his fingers slackened and his knees weakened until they buckled under his weight.

Before Traian hit the rocky floor, large talons grabbed him around the waist and swept him up. His knife fell with a clang that echoed through the vast chamber. Shame filled his limp body. He didn't stand a chance against the beast or the sorceress. He had fallen like a fly being swatted away. *Is this how my sisters and brothers had met their end when the savages came for our village?* No, they must have been braver than him. They would have fought to the death. That is what he chose to believe. He'd seen their bodies strewn across the village square. The only reason he still lived was luck.

Luck may have a had a hand in this, Hunter, but you are destined for greater things. The creature's voice echoed through his skull. *You are much braver than you believe.*

"Get out of my head." Traian gasped. The being set him down on the hard, stone floor but did not release him.

You have great spirit. You will be a strong warrior, but there is much you must learn.

Traian shut his eyes tight, as if that would block the creature's voice. Why had he left the warm hall of the festival? He should have skipped the merriment altogether and stayed in his burdei, sharpening his arrows and knives. *So the legends were true, the stories real.* Either that, or madness had taken over his mind. He'd seen Evelina work her magic through the village mending wounds, calming ailments, serving her people. *She couldn't be so bad, if she was helping, and doing good.* Now he lay at the mercy of this demon-like creature, who Evelina seemed to care about.

You and I need to have a conversation, Hunter. There are many things I must show you and then you can decide for yourself what you will do, what course of action you will take.

The large beast opened its massive wings, filling most of the cavern with red, scaly leather. *A dragon.* Traian's mind flashed back to the festival where Evelina had created a red dragon of fire. He now knew her inspiration. How could she possibly be keeping the people safe with this beast hidden here in the mountains outside the village? What was she thinking? But as he questioned her reasoning, he could almost touch the close magic bond between them. He didn't fully trust Evelina; how could he trust this creature?

You must trust. As promised I will not harm you, but I must warn you. The things I shall show you may disturb you greatly. Alas, they must be seen so you may understand what is at risk.

Traian didn't have much choice. His body continued to betray him and he couldn't lift an arm to swing a punch if he wanted to. *Pathetic.* With a sigh of resignation, he gave the dragon a slight nod.

Evelina spoke from the shadows. "I'll be right here."

He closed his eyes, and in the next moment he was transported to his village… as it was before the raid. From this vantage, he noted his small home at the edge of town. He could see his sisters washing the bedding outside the hut in the midday sun. A pang of grief sliced through his chest, red hot, knowing what was to come, that he could not stop it.

The light changes and it's almost dark. The bell rings, and screams begin. Fires erupt, starting at the south end of the village. Riders on savage-looking beasts clad in black surround the houses. Archers with arrows of flame line behind them and fire the darts into grass roofs. Within moments, he can hear the crackling of the wooden structures succumbing to the heat. People run out of their homes, out into the main square.

Then the beasts let out a bone-chilling screech and burst through the wooden fences surrounding the village. He watches in horror as his people are slaughtered by the axes of the riders and shredded into pieces by the claws and teeth of the beasts. The ground stains red. When Traian is sure he can't take any more, black winged creatures appear out of the dusky sky and begin feasting on the mutilated flesh. Sucking sounds fill the air as they drink the blood pooling around the corpses. A few damned souls manage to fight off some of the beasts, but they are no match for the winged creatures. Fanged mouths rip out the throats of the last remaining men. In all the chaos, he doesn't see his family. But he doesn't need to witness their deaths. He'd already seen what was left of their bodies.

The beasts with their riders, the archers and the winged creatures, leave the decimated village and turn southward from whence they came.

Traian's vision darkens and fades. A soft hand slips into his as he loses consciousness. He woke up with a vengeance, leaping to his feet and ready to fight. Evelina sat on a pillow next to the bed he'd been lying on and watched him with intensity. The tapestry hanging over the entrance of the small space told him they were in one of the cave's many nooks.

"Don't look at me that way, witch," he growled at her. He needed to be strong and not give into her power.

"I can assure you, I am not using any magic. There is no need." She pulled out his hunter's knife and twirled the blade in her hand.

"Give me that." He launched at her, knocking her onto her back. He gripped the wrist of the hand that held his blade.

"What will you do now, Hunter?" she asked in a playful tone.

Her question both calmed and infuriated him in one breath. He didn't intend to hurt her, but that didn't mean he wasn't angry that she'd tricked him into coming here, used magic on him, introduced him to a creature of nightmares, and showed him the destruction of his village. Someone had to pay for the travesties committed against his people. Traian looked down at her face under him and searched her green eyes. Evelina hadn't really fooled him. He'd followed her willingly. And as promised she'd shown him something. He'd expected some magical display of her power, but seeing what had really happened to his village was something he hadn't prepared for.

The warmth of her soft body lying beneath him relaxed the tension in his shoulders. He let go of her wrist and shifted his body next to her. She sat up and handed him his blade. "Here, this belongs to you, and I trust you."

He shook his head. "I don't trust myself."

She set the blade next to him and folded her hands in her lap, holding space for him to speak. The scenes he'd witnessed played through his mind, and the sick feeling in his stomach returned. All he wanted to do was annihilate those who had destroyed his life and family. He wanted revenge. A new heat of anger swept over him and he narrowed his eyes at her.

"How could you watch such a thing and not do something about it?" His jaw tightened as the words left his mouth.

Before she could answer him, the dragon stuck his head through the opening and spoke. "We weren't there. What you saw was only a memory that I tapped into from another dragon's recollections. He was much too strong and dark, but he let me inside his mind and I could see what he saw during the raid."

"He was one of them?" Traian asked as he jumped to his feet, reality sinking in. "There are more of you?"

"Only one other." The dragon's eyelids dropped down. Traian sensed the sadness radiating from them.

Evelina stood up and approached the dragon. "Oh, Zara, you are not alone. You will always have me. I will be with you until the end." She rested her cheek in between the dragon's nostrils.

"I know, dear companion." She huffed a soft breath of warmth.

The gentle intimacy between them struck a chord in Traian's soul. How could a woman be so kind to this creature of nightmares, and this dragon so tender to her in return? The bond between them was undeniable. The connection radiated through him as if he had intruded upon something very personal.

Evelina pushed gently away from the dragon and turned to him. "I ask you again, Hunter. What will you do?"

"I want revenge upon those responsible." A simple answer, but there was more. "And I don't want this to ever happen again."

"Good." She patted Zara's nose. "There is much work to be done then."

Zara growled in agreement. "Indeed."

Evelina returned to Traian, picked up his blade, and put it in his hand. "My dear Hunter, you have much to learn. You have seen what we are up against. I have been able to protect my people thus far, but I fear I cannot do this alone any longer."

"Their masses are growing," hissed Zara.

"I've managed to keep us hidden in this valley, but it's only a matter of time." She released his hand and stepped back. "I need you. We need you. These *people* need you and your fighting spirit."

"And your pure heart," added Zara.

He turned to Zara and frowned. "Pure heart? I was about to slice your throat earlier!"

Zara lifted her scaled head toward the center of the vast cavern and let out a laugh that caused the entire mountain to rumble. "You only proved you were willing to fight."

"Well, who wouldn't fight?" Traian muttered.

Evelina answered, "Most run away from Zara, which is why we avoid humans. They cannot handle the truth anymore."

"What about your people?" Traian asked, putting his knife away, "What do *they* think about Zara?"

"This generation does not know her. We've kept it that way. Best to let them think dragons are only creatures of legend."

This generation? How old is she? Traian shook his head. He honestly didn't want to know. He had enough on his mind to process.

Zara returned her head to their level. "We don't want to draw attention."

"How can you live here idly while people are being slaughtered around you?" Another surge of anger erupted inside him.

Sensing his rage, Evelina held up her hand. "We are not. That is why you are here. Thank the Goddess you followed the buck to us. The time to plan is over. We must now build an army to fight with us, which is why you are here."

The buck. He had followed it for days until he'd reached the top of the ridge from the south. Then it had disappeared without a single trace. *That's how they led me here.* "But I am a hunter, not a warrior."

"Oh, but you will be soon," Evelina said, giving his forearm a gentle squeeze.

As she withdrew her hand, he grabbed her arm and pulled her to him. "How so?"

She leaned into him and lowered her voice. "I will train

you."

Now it was his turn to laugh. "You?" His laughter was cut short in the next moment, as he found himself on his back, with his hunter's blade at his throat. It was Evelina who straddled him. His head stuck out of the cave nook into the open cavern.

"You cheated."

"Tsk, tsk, there was no magic used here, Hunter." Her lips curled into a smirk. "But I can teach you all about magic and how to harness the elements and manipulate the physical world around you, if you are willing."

Zara's chuckle rumbled through the cave. "You indeed have much to learn, Hunter."

Once again, he'd been thrown off his guard by this woman. He didn't like the power she had over him. This was beyond magic. Her strength, beauty, and wit made him want many things he never thought possible, considering recent events. Sure, he'd thought about coupling with one of the lasses from the village he'd seen, but nothing ever came of it. The pairing would have been out of survival and primal need, but what he felt for Evelina was something much different.

Even now, with her on top of him and his own knife at

his throat, the heat inside him was a mix of anger and something white hot. Maybe he wanted her because she presented a unique challenge, or maybe because she ignited feelings inside him he'd never felt before. She scared the marrow out of his bones, yet he wanted nothing more than to be with her. All of the emotions he'd experienced in this short course of time had exhausted his spirit.

Traian shifted under Evelina to look at Zara. "Why did you wait this long to tell me all of this?"

The dragon released a puff of smoke from her nostrils with a snort. "Ask her."

Evelina sighed when he returned his gaze to her. "I wasn't sure. I'm still not. But she thinks you are the one and I trust her."

"I need to get myself some supper. I shall leave you children to your games." Zara angled her wings downward and launched up towards the roof of the cavern. *We'll talk soon, Hunter.*

Traian watched the large creature disappear through a wide slit in the side of the rock. Without the dragon's body's warmth in the cave, he felt the temperature plummet... with the exception of the heat coming from the body straddling his.

I wonder what Zara eats? He probably didn't want to know.

In one graceful movement, Evelina sprang to her feet and offered him her hand. He refused and stumbled to stand in front of her. She once again handed him his knife. He took it, and this time he saw his opportunity. With a twist of his arm, he whirled her around, pinned her back to his chest, and set his blade to her throat. He had no intention of hurting her but since she'd already made an example of him — twice — it was his turn to play.

"Feisty," Evelina purred against his neck.

"How does it feel?" he whispered in her ear.

"You tell me." With a stomp on his left foot, an elbow to his ribs, a kick to the knee, and a quick turn of her body, she pushed back and wrenched the arm holding the knife away from her, knocking it out of his hand with one solid blow to his wrist. He didn't have time to register what was happening before he was chest down on the floor, her foot on the back of his neck, and his arm held up behind him at an impossible angle.

"Good gods." Traian heaved, struggling to breathe. "How did you do that?"

"Years of training. I know you think I'm beneath you

because I am a woman, but I come from a long line of warriors. I can hold my own."

"I can see that."

She pressed her foot down harder. "Which is why I must train you."

Traian gasped. "Okay. I give up. Train me."

"Good." She stepped away, releasing his arm.

He got up to his hands and knees. When he'd walked into this cave he'd been a proud hunter, full of rage, and an appetite of lust. Now he knelt on the stone floor of the cave, broken by a woman and her dragon. Any self-worth or respect had long since vanished. Yet, before tonight, he'd felt powerless against the savages that had killed his people, and rather a coward for hiding in this valley. But the same woman who seemed hellbent on breaking him had also been the first person to give him hope. If he could fight half as good as she could, maybe he did stand a chance of exacting the revenge he so desired. This gave him strength in his bones, enough to stand and face her… despite the pain in his body.

She stepped up to him. "This will only happen if you are willing to trust me." Evelina said, searching out his eyes. "We cannot work together if we cannot trust each other."

"I can *learn* to trust you, but I am afraid I cannot trust my own heart."

"Oh?" She raised an eyebrow.

"I am feeling things I do not understand, things I have never felt before… for anyone. Perhaps it is not my heart, but my nature as a man. I am afraid this may become problematic if we continue to work so close."

She inched nearer until their bodies were touching. "Traian, there is one thing you should trust above all else, and that is your heart," she said, placing her hand on his chest. "Your heart will never mislead you."

He laid his hand over hers. They stared into each other's eyes as a mutual understanding passed between them. Time froze for a moment. This was the beginning of something much larger than them. A silent contract formed between the pair. At that moment, he knew he would give his life for her, and she for him. He felt a spark of fire at the center of his palm where it touched the back of her hand. Traian looked down and lifted his hand away from Evelina's. White shimmering light swirled like a small winter blizzard at the center of his palm. She pulled her hand away from his chest and stepped back, eyes as wide as river boulders.

"It's true," she whispered.

"Are you doing this?" he asked.

"No. You are the one," she said, covering her mouth with the same hand that had been over his heart. "She was right all along."

"Who?"

Evelina now cupped both hands under his. "Zara."

"The dragon?"

"Yes. Zara had a vision of you last summer. She said you would come from the south to seek shelter, and you would be the Bringer of the Light."

"That is why she sent the buck?" The shimmers of light continued to dance within his palm.

"Yes." Evelina gently folded his finger around the flame, forming a fist. Streams of light escaped from the spaces between his fingers. "Traian, you must hold on to this light." She put his fist over his heart. "Never let this fire die within your heart. Dark times are coming and we will need this light to keep us from losing our way."

Speechless, Traian stood staring at the fading streams of light escaping his fist. When he opened his hand again, the flame was gone. Sadness replaced the wonder he'd felt earlier. Evelina took his hand. "We've done enough here tonight. Let us return to the festivities and celebrate."

Being surrounded by people was the last thing Traian desired, but his body wanted to be close to Evelina, and if that meant merriment and revelry, so be it. Plus, he'd certainly had his fill of the supernatural for tonight. Perhaps being around common folk was a fine idea after all. He squeezed her hand. "Only if you promise not to ask me to dance."

"Pff, not a chance. Yule's Eve dance is mandatory."

Hand in hand, they exited the cave the same way they had entered. Evelina's free hand held the red flame that lit their way back. The snowfall had stopped, leaving the entire forest surrounding the town in a white blanket of diamonds that sparkled in the torchlight at the entrance of the village.

Traian stopped her before she opened the white door. "I never thought you were beneath me," he said, his eyes searching hers.

She didn't say anything.

"I just wanted to clear that up."

Evelina nodded. "Very well, it's cleared. Can we go in now?"

"The light back there," he pointed in the direction of the cave, "the light in my palm. Does that mean I am magic too?"

She closed her hand to extinguish the flame and she patted his cheek. "Everyone is magic. Now let's go inside before we turn into magical ice figures."

"Very well."

He pulled the door open and they entered the great hall. The festival carried on as if nothing strange had happened. Men, women, and children all danced around the fire hearth at the center of the large room. "Are you ready?" Evelina leaned into him.

"For what?"

"The dance."

"Remember, I don't dance."

"Nonsense." She laughed, pulling him into the throng of people. They clasped hands with another couple on either side, forming a line that spun around the fire. His feet moved quickly to the beat of the drum, kicking up in the air with every high note, keeping in time with the other men around the dance circle.

Round and round they danced. Traian laughed and

enjoyed himself for the first time in many moons. He felt real joy in his heart. In the merriment, he forgot about all the horrors and strange phenomena he'd witnessed earlier. With Evelina at his side, Traian allowed himself to take a break and relish the good things in life — spiced cake, ale, children's laughter, and dancing with a fetching woman. He never thought he would ever enjoy dancing but he did.

They cycled again through the dance ring, then stood off to the side of the room, admiring the greenery. He looked up and recognized the foliage hanging directly above their heads. Without wasting another second, he cupped her face and kissed the lips he'd fancied since the moment he'd laid eyes on her. To his surprise, they softened against his. He'd expected to be thrown onto his back at any minute, but instead she wrapped her arms around his waist.

"Took you long enough," she said against his lips before kissing him back.

***

Traian opened his eyes. He could still taste the spiced cake from her lips. He checked at his hand, the one that had held the white light so long ago. The rich aromas of herbs and spices from the crone's brewed concoctions filled his nose, replacing the fir, lavender, and rosemary. His beat-less heart ached. Countless years had gone by since that beautiful night. He'd do anything to go back; to hold the light again… to hold her again.

"Take heart, son," the crone said from the darkened corner of her hut, "you'll see her again."

"You say this every time." His voice was but a whisper as his body lay weakened.

"I say it, because it's true. She is coming. I can feel her."

He desperately wanted to believe the old witch's words, yet doubt overruled any spark of hope that may have existed in his dark heart.

"You will see the light again," Satra said. He hadn't seen or sensed her move next to him, but she touched his ashen face with her weathered hand. "I promise." She took his hand. "You *will* hold the light again."

For the first time in the two centuries he'd been visiting the crone, he chose to believe her.

To Be Continued

Spring Fever
A Legends of Carpatia Tale

This story is dedicated to my husband. Love you, babe

•

Chapter 1

Traian stood at the base of the snowy mountain, staring at the jagged rocky surface. Moonlight glittered on the snow-covered crags and peaks. He'd been here countless times, searching. Time had changed the landscape. Where he stood, an ancient forest had once towered over him. At the center of the valley, there'd been a thriving village he'd called home, until it too was destroyed, along with everything he loved. Alpine grass and barren rocks now covered where a dozen thatch-roofed, burdei-style homes once stood. When he closed his eyes, he could smell the burning hearths of the people he long ago vowed to protect.

Somewhere there was an entrance into the mountain, and this time he wouldn't leave until he found it. Ever since last Yule, a new determination fueled his quest to find anything that could link him to his past, and to Evelina. He'd spent many nights at the Romanian Archaeological Institute in Cluj, searching all the old maps in their archives. He'd visited the Geological Center of Romania in Bucharest and studied every diagram and aerial photo of the Carpathian Mountains. Nothing indicated the presence of a cave where he'd spent quality time with a very crafty little sorceress and her fiery dragon eons ago.

Instead of relying solely on his strigoi senses, he had a new device, the latest in geologic surveying according to the professor at the university. He pulled it from his leather satchel and turned it on. He scanned the mountain from right to left, a beep sounding intermittently. Over and over he scanned and after five hours and two battery packs, the mountain had been thoroughly checked several times, but with no results.

"Shit," he mumbled under his breath and threw the device at the mountain. *Now what?*

Not a single trace of a crack or opening remained. Ever since his master had released him, he'd been searching for clues to his past, something that was forbidden in strigoi law, the law his master had enforced. Earthquakes, landslides, and floods had changed the lay of the land. The magic that once existed here had long dried up. He'd hoped to tap into the ancient energy that had flowed freely, but he found nothing.

Traian knelt on the icy ground. Spring wouldn't arrive in the Carpathian Mountains until after Summer Solstice, but even then, many of the snowfields remained the entire year.

He massaged his chin as he sat back on his heels and watched pieces of the scanner fall down the mountain.

He listened as the debris found its final resting place in the gorge below, his hyper-sensitive ears picking up every scuffle made by rock and metal touching. Everything was quiet except for the occasional icy gust whistling down the slopes. He stood up, his broad shoulders slouched. *Maybe I should bring Satra here.* He brushed the thought away. The old gypsy witch's health had taken a dive since his last visit. She wouldn't be able to handle the cold or terrain and if she died here, that would give the nomadic magic folk the excuse they needed to start a war with the strigoi. He turned back down the path.

Drip. Drip. Drip.

He stopped short. He knew that sound. The echo that followed the water droplet falling from the rock ceiling and hitting the cave floor almost made his heart start beating again. His bat-like wings sprung out from the folds of his leather coat and he took flight, following the sound. On a section of the mountainside covered with boulders from a century's old landslide, he landed on one of the large rocks and focused on the dripping water. This *was* the spot. With one smooth motion, he gripped the boulder above him and yanked it over his shoulder, as if it were a deflated soccer ball.

One by one, Traian removed the years of fallen rock, but a cascade of boulders tumbled over the space left by every rock he removed. He didn't seem to notice. This was his first lead since the couple of collapsed tunnels he'd found two decades earlier.

Hours later, after moving what felt like half of the mountain with his bare hands, an opening large enough to squeeze through emerged. Traian retracted his wings and snaked his body through the small hole into the dark, dragging his satchel behind him. As the light faded, his night vision activated. Five meters from the entrance, the narrow tunnel widened. He moved from a belly crawl to knees and hands. Traian felt the grooves in the rock. A sudden heaviness in his chest caused him to stop. He closed his eyes. *Zara.* The beautiful, red-scaled dragon filled his vision. Traian could almost feel her presence now, even though she'd been dead almost four thousand years. The last of her kind. If only he could hear her thunderous growl once again. His fingers traced over the indentations made by her mighty talons. A chill of excitement spread over his body. *This was it.*

Traian opened his eyes and crawled a few more meters until the ceiling heightened enough for him to stand. He studied the rock surface above and moved forward until he came to a massive blockage of rocks where the ceiling had collapsed.

"Damn it." Traian spat to the side and rolled his shoulders, preparing for another round of digging.

The wounds on his hands from the last stint had already healed. This time, he cleared the path faster. Before long, he'd reached the end of the tunnel, which opened into a vast cavern. Traian stared up at the impossibly high ceiling, the walls of the cavern receding into the darkness, obscuring the far side. Incredibly, it had not caved in like the smaller tunnels leading in. He leapt down off the ledge, landing lightly on the balls of his feet. From the leather bag, he pulled out a flare, lit it, and tossed it into the round, concave area at the center of the cavern that Zara had once used as her bed. The room lit up in the red glow of the flames. It wasn't the same light that Evelina had produced with a snap of her finger, but it would have to do.

Many of the sconces were still fastened to the walls of the cave, although none of them had seen a flame in thousands of years. He reached out and touched the concha shell fossil embedded into the rock, a smile spreading across his face. A sudden cracking sound in the ceiling caught his attention, but before he could react, a small boulder struck the side of his head. Dazed, he fell to the hard ground face first, his vision blurring.

Chapter 2

Traian's vision cleared, and he groaned as his back hit the rock floor for the fiftieth time.

"Up." Evelina heaved, catching her breath. "No time for rest."

The previous two months of training hadn't done him a bit of good when it came to fighting Evelina. He hated this training, not because of the physical strain on his body, but because he *was forced* to fight her. Traian's muscles had increased in size and his skills too, but he couldn't get over his aversion to fighting a woman. Women should be protected, respected, but not sparred with.

"Up." Evelina insisted. "If I were a fiend, I would have ripped your throat out by now."

That gave him the strength to continue this torturous ordeal. Evil lurked south of the mountains, and it would come here, of that he was certain. Traian glanced down at his hand, willing to glimpse the flame of light he'd seen on Yule's Eve, but it hadn't returned since, which made him wonder if it had been a trick of light or just a fluke. He picked up his sword and readied for the next round.

Evelina leaned against the wall, her shoulders rising and falling with each labored breath. He'd never seen her out of breath before.

"Evelina," he said, stepping closer and lowering his sword, "are you all right?"

"Aye, just a little tired. I didn't sleep well last night," she replied, her weak smile forced. He noticed a layer of moisture covering her skin. Evelina never perspired.

"You don't look well." Traian reached out to her, but she swatted his hand away.

"Enough. I'm fine. We need to keep practicing," she said and walked to the center of the training area. "From the beginning. Charge me."

Traian closed his eyes and repeated the movements she'd rehearsed with him. *Find her weak spot, but aim for a different area until the last moment and then strike.* He opened his eyes and zeroed in on her narrow waist, but then drew his attention to her chest. Drops of sweat trickled from her neck and disappeared into the white and silver corset covering her breasts.

"Traian, we do not have all day," she said through gritted teeth.

He charged, swinging his sword. Metal clanged as her blade met his, echoing through the vast cavern. Without hesitation, he pivoted his knee into the side of her hip, knocking her off balance. She stepped back, quickly regaining her footing, and swung her sword at him. He blocked it, but the velocity of her strike jerked him back a step. Evelina swiped at him again, and he blocked her sword, but not the fierce kick to the back of his knee. Traian didn't even have time to stop his fall.

On and on the pair sparred. Each time Traian went down, he found it harder to get back up, yet Evelina pressed on despite the paleness of her face and heavy breathing. He'd never seen her like this before. He stood up and advanced on her once more, matching her moves. She moved back and he swung at her again. She didn't block, but jumped out of the way, avoiding his blow. He pressed forward until she'd reached the wall with her hand, attempting to hold on to the concha shell embedded in the cave wall, but fell to her knees.

"I need to rest," Evelina gasped, and he watched her eyes roll back into their sockets. Dropping his sword, Traian caught her before she collapsed to the floor.

"Evelina." Traian shouted, shaking her limp body.

"No, no, no! Wake up. Evelina!" He panicked. He kissed her forehead. Her skin burned. *Fever.*

He believed since she could heal the ailments of the villagers, she could resist any disease. Yet here she lay in his arms, her body hot like a summer fire. He pressed his ear to her chest and sighed in relief. Shallow breath still flowed in her lungs, her heart beating like a weak drum. He didn't know what to do. He needed Zara. As if she'd heard his inner plea, the dragon appeared through the opening high above them. She glided down with her large, bat-like wings, landing gently on the cavern floor.

"Help her," Traian implored.

"Step aside," Zara ordered.

He didn't want to let go of the woman who had claimed his heart, but he laid her down on the rock floor to give the dragon ample room. Zara stepped forward, lowering her massive head to sniff Evelina's body. She closed her eyes, examining the scent of her companion. A moment later she opened her eyes and growled.

"She's been poisoned." Zara hissed. "What did she eat and drink today?"

"I do not know," Traian said, shaking his head. "I did not break bread with her today."

"When did she fall?"

"A few moments ago," Traian answered, "She's been acting strangely during our training session. I managed to knock her back a couple of times, which you know never happens. And she was sweating."

Zara whirled around and pounced into the dining cove, knocking over pots and jars. He could hear ceramic smashing onto the floor.

Aargh!

The dragon's roar extinguished all the torches and sconces within the cave. Even Traian's hair blew away from his face. The only light inside the cavern came from the enraged dragon's glowing, ruby scales covering her large body.

"Blasted beetle brains," Zara growled, her head swung around to face Traian. She held a small jar in her teeth, which she set down at his feet. "How did this get here?"

He picked up the vessel, smelled its contents, and recoiled. The pungent odor of the cider vinegar Evelina drank each day filled his nostrils. The liquid appeared like blood in the dragon's firelight.

"I do not know," Traian said, shaking his head. "She insisted on drinking that wretched stuff."

"It's been poisoned." Zara roared and stomped her foot, causing the cave to rumble. "How did the poison get in here, Hunter?"

"I do not know!" Traian shouted. "Haven't you been listening? We did not break bread together today. I have no idea what she ate or drank." He rushed back to Evelina and placed a hand on her head. "She's getting hotter."

"We need to get her to the pool," Zara bellowed. Pushing Traian to the side with her wings, she scooped Evelina up in one claw and headed down the only tunnel the enormous dragon could fit through.

Traian kept pace behind. He knew where Zara was going and should have taken her there the moment Evelina had collapsed. *Why hadn't I done that?* he thought, angry with himself.

Yes, why indeed? Zara's voice roared inside his skull. He would never get used to the sensation of the dragon inside his head.

Get out. He erected black walls around his mind, just as Evelina had taught him. Learning to shield his mind had been the most challenging task he'd ever experienced, and the only thing he'd managed to improve upon since she'd brought him to this cave last winter.

When they reached the lake chamber, Zara set Evelina down in the shallow water. Traian stood back, not wanting to interfere with things he knew little about. He sat down on a nearby rock, ready to spring up at a moment's notice.

Traian watched in horror as Zara took Evelina's entire head into her mouth. His mental guards came down. He was about to pull out his hunter's blade. *Stand down, Hunter. She is safe.* His hand didn't leave the handle of the knife, but he relaxed back a little. Zara and Evelina had a magical bond, this he knew. If one died, the other would shortly follow, and they protected each other fiercely. Even with this knowledge, he couldn't stop the unease creeping up his spine as he watched the woman of his heart disappear halfway into the dragon's mouth.

After several agonizingly long moments, Zara opened her mouth, letting Evelina slide back into the water. The sight made him swallow down the bile that had unexpectedly risen. The beast let out a deafening roar, which caused a couple of stalactites to come crashing down into the underground lake. The dragon leapt out of the water and landed in front of Traian, her eyes glowing with fire.

"It's up to you, Hunter." She lowered her head until they were seeing each other at eye level. "She's been poisoned with magic so strong that even I can't pull it out of her body."

"Magic?"

"Yes, Hunter. Stay with her while I examine the source once more." Before Traian could respond, the dragon had already disappeared down the tunnel they'd just come in through. The speed of everything happening had his head reeling.

The only light inside the cave were two glowing white staffs marking the entrance. It would have been most beautiful he'd seen had the image not been tainted by the fact that Evelina's life stood on death's threshold. The creamy laced top and dress she wore glowed against the dark water. Her golden hair framed her ivory face and rosy lips had turned an ashen violet. Traian thought perhaps it was the cold water, but when he touched her skin, the fever raged on within her body. He knew she was still alive. Barely. He knelt into the frigid water next to her and stroked the side of her face. All he wanted was to cradle her small body in his arms and kiss her purple lips.

Do not kiss her lips! The poison could kill you on contact. Zara's voice boomed inside his head as if she were next to him.

He kissed Evelina's forehead instead. "Please stay with us," he whispered. "I cannot lose you. We need you. I need you." Traian held her in his arms, ignoring the numbness creeping up his legs from the icy water.

Zara's thunderous steps announced her return. "Nightshade mixed with black magic. She has only hours, perhaps a day, to live. Had it been only nightshade, I could have pulled it out of her blood, but the magic is infusing the poison into her organs faster than I can remove it without draining her life force. It is up to you then, Hunter, to save her."

Traian pulled Evelina closer to his body. "Me? If you can't help her, what could I possibly do?"

"Hidden in the mists of the mountains lies a world of magic concealed from the human eye." Zara stepped into the water. "You must go to the portal, enter the Otherworld, get a petal of the moonstone flower that grows in the elven temple garden in Transpatia."

"Have you gone mad?" He spat in disbelief.

"There is no time." Zara said, reaching for her companion with a wing. "I will take you to the mountain where the portal is located, but I can't follow you in."

"Why didn't Evelina speak of this Transpatia?" Traian reluctantly released Evelina back to Zara.

"She had her reasons." Zara took Evelina into her talons and cradled her body with a wing. "We must leave now."

"But, I don't know where I'm going, or what I'm looking for," Traian protested, stepping out of the water and onto the rocks, his legs numb from the cold. "How do I get in?"

"You will find a way. You are clever, Hunter. We must go now. I will do everything I can to keep her alive until you have accomplished this mission." Zara stared at him. "It's up to you. If she dies, we all die."

Traian felt as if all his blood had drained to his numb feet while his head spun at the new information. Of course, there was an Otherworld. Why should he be surprised? If dragons existed, why not elves and woodland folk? But he couldn't help feeling betrayed by Evelina for withholding this information from him. He steadied himself by leaning against the wall of the cave, realizing why Zara couldn't leave. The dragon was the only magical creature that could continue to channel Evelina's spells and keep the protective shield over the village.

Zara released Evelina into the water again and took a deep breath. When she exhaled, a long tongue of fire came out of her mouth. He watched as the red flame curled around Evelina repeatedly, wrapping her in a fiery cocoon. A glass case enclosed his love as the fire dissipated. "Let us go." Zara jumped to the shore and lowered her long neck to the ground. When he didn't move, she hissed, "You're wasting precious time, boy. Hop on."

Chapter 3

His hands clenched for a moment. The day couldn't get any stranger. He'd never ridden Zara before. Not once since Yule's Eve had Evelina or Zara offered him a jaunt on the magical beast. He didn't realize how much he appreciated that until now when fear froze him. However, this was not the time to cower. He tightened his jaw and leapt onto Zara's back, narrowly avoiding being impaled by the spikes lining her spine.

Without a moment to settle himself, the dragon surged forward. Traian caught a fleeting glance of Evelina over his shoulder before he shot through the tunnel with Zara. He didn't have time to get comfortable with the idea of traveling to a magical land or riding a dragon and this went against his calculated, hunter ways.

He gripped the spikes on Zara's back tightly as the dragon took flight to the high slit in the wall of the main cave. Within two breaths, they burst from the mountain and into the sky. Below he could see the village tucked away in the middle of the forest valley. He spotted the golden sphere covering the settlement. *Evelina's magic fence.* The awe-inducing sight quickly transformed into shock as he witnessed small patches of the barrier dissolving before his eyes.

"Her magic is weakening," Zara roared as they soared higher and away from the scene. "We have only hours."

He knew what that meant. The pressure grew with each heartbeat, but he felt no closer to the solution than he had when Evelina had collapsed. How could he find this flower and get back in time? What was this Otherworld like? How far was the Elven temple? What did it look like? What if he lost his way?

Fear not, Hunter. Zara's voice rumbled through his head. *You will find the moonstone flower.*

How can you be certain? Traian asked.

Zara chuckled. *I know. Dragons always know.*

He held on for dear life as they flew deeper and higher into the mountains. Soon they were surrounded by clouds, but Zara continued, seeming to know exactly where they were going. Moments later they were at the base of a large mountain. Zara landed and Traian hopped off her scaly back. His legs felt weak, but he was glad to be on solid ground once again.

"You will find the portal at the top of this mountain,

inside of a cave. It's not unlike our cavern back home. This is as far as I can take you," Zara said. "I must return to Evelina. We are exposed enough as it is."

Traian looked at the looming mountain. "There is much ground to cover."

"Agreed. First, I must give you something." Zara dipped her head to the ground and made a horrid retching sound. She coughed several times, and then stuck her tongue out at him.

At the tip of her tongue, she held a silver chain with a glass vial. *Take it.* Zara stretched her it to him. *Put the petal of moonstone flower inside this to it carry back.*

"Where did you—"Traian stopped the question. He didn't really want to know, nor did he want to waste any more time. He took the chain and put it over his head, tucking the vial under his tunic. The metal and glass felt dry and warm against his skin.

"Be safe, Hunter." Zara nudged him with her nose. "Her life depends on your success."

Before he could touch her with his hand, she whirled around and sprang into the air. "Two more things, Hunter. Elves are never what they appear. And don't mention dragons when you cross over." She disappeared into the clouds surrounding the mountain.

Traian concentrated on the steep mountain and started climbing. The wind blew around him, cutting through his training clothes and down to his bones. In the chaos, he'd forgotten his cloak, and his boots and trousers were still wet. Like all the mountains in Carpatia, snow covered this one too. *If I'm still in Carpatia.*

Alone and cold, the mission seemed more daunting than ever. He kept climbing because movement distracted him from the cold. Adrenaline and his recent training with Evelina helped him ascend faster than he'd anticipated. One foot in front of the other gave way to leaps from rock to rock. To his amazement, the higher he climbed the easier the effort became. Despite the lightness of foot, the fate of Evelina and the village hung heavy on his shoulders. Everyone was already in great danger. Someone outside of the village knew of Evelina and her magic. This concerned him greatly, especially now that he wasn't there to protect her. *She has Zara,* he reminded himself. No one in their right mind would muddle with a dragon. But then he recalled the bond — if Evelina died, Zara would too.

Evelina, the people, and Zara depend on this mission. On me. This reminder spurred him up the mountain. He had his blade and that was all he really needed. The mountain disappeared into another layer of clouds. He could barely see anything, but pressed on. Before he realized where he was he had reached the top. There, mostly hidden by the mist, he spotted an entrance to a cave. Without hesitation, he entered, expecting to be swallowed in darkness. Instead, light shone brightly down illuminating his feet. Traian lifted his hand where a white flame danced in his palm. He sighed a moment of relief.

The cave opened a short distance later onto another mountainside, mirror image to the one he had climbed. Gone were the clouds as bright sunshine lit the valley before him. The mountains descended into rolling hills, forests, meadows, fields, lakes, rivers, and a sea at the furthest his eyes could see. Nothing resembled a settlement or civilization. He turned to the cave from which he'd come. Above the snowy entrance a green stone glowed in the sunlight. He hoped it was a good omen. However, the white flame in his palm had disappeared.

The sun hung high in the sky. *Noon.* His stomach growled in response. The food he'd devoured for breakfast had long been consumed by his body. *Had that only been this morning?* Traian felt as if he'd lived several lifetimes since. He had to keep moving, so he jumped down a few rocks from the entrance and surveyed the land again, this time paying attention to all the detail. Just as before, the only life below was the same as the life on the human side minus the stormy clouds hiding the sawtooth crags.

He descended as quickly as possible without falling. When he reached the bottom of the mountain, the greenest grass he'd ever seen replaced the snow. He was wrong, the life here was nothing like on the human side. Everything had a brighter shade or hue. Grass gleamed in the sunlight as if tiny gems had been sprinkled onto its blades. The bark on the trees shone as if covered with rare ambers. Various shades of green adorned the trees as they swayed in the gentle breeze. The cold air of the mountain had vanished and warmth wrapped his body like a wool cloak, as if he'd stepped right into summer. Flowers of every color peppered the forest floor like jewels of a crown. Traian felt his body relax and his knees weakened to the point where he dropped down to the grass. His eyelids drooped with heaviness. Perhaps he could lie down for a moment. He needed strength after all, so a little rest wouldn't hurt. He sat down and leaned his back against the trunk of a tree. *Just for a moment.* He yawned and closed his eyes.

A soft bed of moss cradling him was the last thing Traian remembered, until something sharp poked him in the ribs. He tried to bat it away, but someone's boot pressed his hand to the ground. When he opened his eyes to find many white faces, peering down at him. Traian tried to sit up, but his body was being forced down. His heart drummed wildly in his chest.

Chapter 4

How long have I been asleep? Where am I? Who are these people? He studied at the faces through squinted eyes. It didn't take him very long to see a resemblance. Everything made sense why Evelina had always kept her distance from him. Save a few kisses they shared, their affection had never progressed further. At first, he'd thought it was because she didn't fancy him, but sometimes he clearly saw lust in her eyes, yet she always held back, never giving into the intimacy they both craved. Her eyes, the curve of her lips, high cheekbones, all reflected in the faces around him. Evelina had always kept her ears hidden behind her cornsilk hair. *Evelina is an elf,* he thought, as bitterness filled his mouth.

He'd never known an elf before. His right hand tingled again, as it had at the portal on the mountain. He tried to raise his hand to show them, but a spear blocked his forearm.

Faces changed from that of curiosity to suspicion, and he listened to footsteps approaching. The feet that held him down moved. As Traian tried to sit up, he realized he couldn't move his body. *Fool.* He recognized the feeling, knowing it very well as his training came to mind. Black walls went up sealing his mind away from the minds meddling with his. The flame within his right hand grew larger. If only he knew how he could use it.

Traian could now move his head, a good sign. He took in the room. The walls were equal part stone and wood. Tall trees created the pillars supporting the walls, and branches from the trees created the windows. The floor was smooth like polished stone.

Returning his attention to his body, he concentrated on expanding the shield to include his frame, pushing away any magic from outside sources. This was a lesson he'd failed each time with Evelina, but she was a much bigger distraction than a handful of armed elves. To his surprise, it worked. He could move and sat up to meet the new elf who had just joined them.

Dressed in emerald green trousers, a deep purple cape, and a leather vest covering his white tunic, this elf appeared different than the rest. On his head, a golden band wrapped his forehead, his blue eyes full of concentration. Traian recognized that look too and took heart that his shield indeed had worked. It was a short victory. His spark of joy came to a halt as he was thrown onto his back again, without anyone laying a hand on him. The flame in his hand extinguished.

Rotten chestnuts. Traian quickly returned the shield to his mind. It was far easier to protect his head than his whole body. Without a word, the elves guarding him began to exit the room, until only he and the distinguished elf remained.

"So, you've come for the moonstone flower?" The elf's voice sounded as smooth and cold as the floor Traian lay on.

"How do you —" But he knew the answer to this question and fell silent again, keeping his concentration and strength on the shield around his mind.

"She taught you well." The elf paced around him and stopped at his side, offering his hand.

Traian avoided the gesture and stood. He didn't know how long he would have control of his body and needed to make sure he was in a better position than with his back on the ground. Now that he was standing, the elf didn't seem so threatening. Traian stood a palm higher than him. "How much do you know?" Traian asked.

"Enough," the elf replied, scanning him from head to toe. "Did you really think you could walk into our world, go to our most sacred place, and steal the rarest flower from us?" The elf's tone reeked of superiority.

Traian suppressed the urge to knock his perfect face

into the stone floor. The elf had already wasted too much precious time. He needed to find the flower and get out of this place, but diplomacy was needed here. If these people were anything like Evelina, they could pound him to a pulp without lifting a finger.

"Let us start from the beginning. How did you find our gate?" the elf demanded.

Traian cocked his head. "What gate?"

"The portal to our world. It's hidden from the human eye."

"I'm a hunter and I live in the mountains."

"Yes, but you are human. You shouldn't be able to see our magic. You walked right in without setting off our alarms. Even our vigilant guards were taken by surprise. It took several strong spells to tranquilize you." The elf began pacing back and forth. "You're still alive, because I am curious. You are a hunter, not a wizard, yet you have magic. Weak magic, I might add. What did Eve give you to help you resist our magic?"

"Eve?"

"Oh yes, what does she call herself now? Evelina?" The elf raised his brow.

Evelina. No matter how grassed he felt about her withholding such vital information from him, her life faded with each passing breath. He needed to get moving. Trying to be as respectful as possible, he spoke, "Look, I don't know who you are, but I want two things to be clear. I mean no harm to anyone, and I need the moonstone flower or she'll die."

"How was she poisoned?"

Traian hated that the elf knew too much and strengthened his shield once more before responding. "I do not know, but it was dark magic."

The elf held an expressionless face, but in his eyes, Traian recognized the concentration he'd seen with Evelina.

"Will you help me?" Traian asked, taking a risk.

"Why should I?" The elf snorted.

"Because her life, and the lives of those she protects, depends on it."

"Humans." The elf spat with disdain. "Why should I help them or her?"

"Because it's the right thing to do."

"What do you know of right? Whose right are we speaking of? What is right for *you* or for us?"

"Right for everyone," Traian's retorted, his voice getting louder. "If you think what happens to us won't affect you, you are gravely mistaken."

"As if you can stand up to us."

"Maybe not," Traian admitted. "But there is evil infecting our land and it will come here too."

"Please don't say that when we take you to the king." The elf stopped and raised an eyebrow. "Oh, and avoid the subject of the dragon. That will get you killed."

They eyed each other for a moment, until suddenly, the wooden door opened and a new set of guards marched in. Traian noted the red dragon crest woven on the chest of their silver tunics. They stood taller than the rest of the elves and bowed their heads briefly to the other elf, and then surrounded Traian.

"The king is ready for you now," the elf said.

Guards escorted Traian out of the room and the elf followed. Traian glanced through the arched windows into the wooded courtyard beyond. The surrounding buildings blended into the forest, as if they had grown along with the trees. A long hallway connected them to a different building where guards lined up on either side of smooth iridescent white doors. The doors didn't appear to be wood or stone, but a blend of the two.

The leading elf motioned for Traian to enter ahead of him, as the doors opened. He strengthened his mental shield once again and tried not to seem too frustrated. He had to win the elves' trust, but keep his mind protected.

He walked into the throne room and focused on his breathing, but the splendor and light caught his breath. The entire room was one gigantic crystal that had been hollowed out to create the king's throne room. Translucent texture of the crystal provided privacy from the outside yet allowed light to stream into the room. Traian sensed the strong energy of the room and the vibration of the crystal through his feet. In his training, Evelina had used crystals to teach him how to channel his internal energy and forces around his body. There were several caves deeper in her lair that contained enormous crystals. He'd enjoyed the crystal work with Evelina, yet here, he felt vulnerable. It was as if the massive energy could be used against him.

Call the earth magic. He heard Evelina's voice in his head as if she were with him. Only a memory, but it was enough. He channeled his mental strength onto the crystal floor and withdrew energy that strengthened his mental shield and body, as Evelina had instructed him. He felt the power of the crystal create an invisible body shield. This crystal was ten times stronger than the ones he'd worked with before. Feeling secure, he turned his attention to the man sitting on the sparkling throne.

The man wore a regal crown and a long silver robe with the red dragon woven on his chest just like the guards who had escorted him there. The seat itself suited the man on it. A rainbow of gemstones and flowers grew from the gleaming floor, their vines tangling with the stones of the throne.

"Welcome, Hunter." The king stood and stepped down off his throne. He extended his arm to Traian.

Traian gripped the king's forearm and bowed his head in respect. "Thank you, sire." When the king did not let go, he focused on the energy shield he'd created moments before, channeling the power of the crystal through his body.

"My, you are strong for a human." The king let go of Traian and threw his arms up in a jovial manner, "Obviously, you've had dealings with our kind because you know how to block us. And well, I might add." He turned to climb back up to his throne.

"I did not know she was of your kind, but she is my teacher," he responded to the unasked question.

"Is she, now?" The king paused and gave him a half-glance and raised eyebrow. Traian recognized that same expression from when Evelina teased or questioned his motives. The king sat back into his grandly adorned chair. "Well, Padrick tells me you are here to procure a sample of moonstone flower."

He glanced at the elf who had led him there. *Padrick.*

He would remember that name. He replayed Padrick's last words in his head before being escorted to the throne room. *I would also avoid the subject of the dragon. That will only get you killed.*

"Your Highness, she will die without it," he said and bowed his head. "I ask you kindly to have mercy on one of your own, and let me take to her what will heal her. She has bestowed much good on my people and I owe this to her."

The king touched his hands together and drew his fingers to his lips. His green eyes stared off into the space between them as if he saw something there that Traian hadn't.

He looked up at Traian as if caught in thought. "I will speak with my council and let you know the decision," the king finally said.

Traian's frustration with the king's answer almost made him lose control over his mental shields. He couldn't afford this delay, but he couldn't afford for his mind to be opened to these mythical creatures. He had to stay focused on his mission.

"Padrick, please escort our guest to the visitor garden." The King ordered. "And please don't let your personal feelings get in the way."

Traian thought about the monarch's last words as the elf guard and Padrick led him into a garden beyond his wildest dreams. Not that he had ever dreamed of gardens, but if he ever had it would pale in comparison to this. Flowers of every color sprang from vines flowing over stone walls and cascading onto the bushes lining a labyrinth of paths. At the center, a grand white fountain bubbled a serene melody. Shiny stones placed in the pathways glowed in the diffuse light. Tall trees surrounded the garden like ancient sentinels keeping guard. Alas, this wasn't the temple garden he'd hoped for. He reached for his neck to touch chain that held the glass vile, but it was gone.

"I shall give you a tour," Padrick said. "But you must stay close to me and do exactly as I tell you." The elf grabbed Traian by the arm. "Here we have the Fountain of Aria, named after the last queen to rule our land. This resting seat was dedicated by the priestess of the Temple of Gaia." He motioned to stone bench carved with ornate design.

Panic sparked at the pit of Traian's stomach as they walked along one of the walls. "Here we have sunbursts." He pointed at the yellow blossoms hanging down the wall. "Stand still."

The elf's voice lowered as he whispered something in a language Traian didn't understand but recognized instantly. This put him on edge, because every time he heard these words, he knew magic was about to happen. Padrick parted the drape of the vines and touched the stone wall behind. Before he could react to any of this, Traian found himself inside a long, dark tunnel, illuminated only by light coming through the cracks in the stone. He glanced back to see himself and Padrick standing in the garden talking as the heavy stone door closed.

"What in the gods'..."

"We must move quickly, don't drop your shield." Padrick cut Traian off and pulled him down through the passageway.

All this rapid change of scenery and situations made Traian feel like the one time he fell off a horse as a kid. The fall had caused him to tumble down a hill. Before he could get his bearings, he had found himself in a mountain stream. This felt like that. Only he was surrounded by people he didn't understand and couldn't quite trust. He trusted Evelina, even though she had withheld this important information, but these elves were of a different realm. He didn't appreciate where his mission was heading.

He and Padrick continued down several connecting tunnels until they reached a door. As Padrick opened it, the wood creaked as if the door hadn't been opened in a long time. They stepped out into the woods. Traian had to blink as his eyes adjusted to the light. He looked around and was surprised to discover that he'd exited out the base of a tree.

"This way." Padrick pulled him deeper into the woods.

"Where are you taking me?" Traian finally asked. "And what did you do back there?"

"We must move quickly." The elf continued to pull him up a wooded hill. "Our aura clones will only last for a short time…that is, if the guards don't come back sooner."

Traian stumbled along, trying to keep up with the elf's rapid pace. His agile movements reminded Traian of Evelina. Now he knew where she got her gracefulness. And beauty. And magic. How had he not noticed this before? He'd known she was special, but then, he didn't know much about the magic world. Obviously.

When they reached a grove of cone-shaped trees, Padrick stopped, closed his eyes, and waved his hands in a spiral motion. He went from tree to tree until he settled at one on the far right. "This way." He motioned to Traian.

Without hesitation, he followed the elf through the tree portal into yet another darkened passageway. He thought this tunnel would never end. It curved to the right and then to the left. Traian's lungs burned from all the exertion. The effort of keeping his mental shield up and trying to maintain pace with a magical being taxed his reserves. He didn't know how much farther he could go. Then he remembered finding the carnage of his home village that morning that seemed both like a lifetime ago and yesterday.

If the Southern Savages had anything to do with Evelina's poisoning, there would be hell to pay. For Evelina, and the people she protected, he would push on. He would get what he'd come for and he would go back and heal her. Traian would step up his training. He would grow his knowledge of magic and make sure she taught him everything she could. He would never feel as helpless as now or when he had found his home burnt to the ground. Traian didn't care he was only human. Humans could be strong and could stand against magic folk.

Stronger now and more in control, he would get through this day and return home. This truth radiated deep in his bones. He didn't trust Padrick, but something about the elven king caused his internal alarm fires to blaze, and the man seemed too friendly. Padrick didn't seem to trust the king either.

Traian kept pace with the elf through the tunnels until Padrick stopped without warning. The elf touched a knotted tree root in front of them. It creaked and groaned until a portal formed. Padrick shot right through. Traian didn't hesitate to follow, gasping when he caught sight of the splendor around him as his eyes adjusted to the light. They had entered another elven garden. This one however, was much larger than the one near the king's throne room, and it was full of crystals. Each cluster had flowers growing around them, matching the color of the gem. Rainbows of light danced everywhere around them. He didn't have to ask because he knew where they were. He had to find the milky-white, iridescent stone, and surely, he would find it here.

"They grow by the north wall." Padrick pointed ahead. With the other hand, he reached inside his tunic and pulled out a chain with the glass vial. "The king would have had your head off, had he seen this."

Traian opened his mouth to ask why, but a loud horn blew in the distance with several more joining a moment later.

Padrick thrust the vial into Traian's hand. "That's the alarm. We do not have much time. You must hurry." The elf stuck two fingers inside his mouth and let out a high-pitched whistle. "What are you waiting for? Go!"

Traian grasped the vial tightly. He would not lose it again. He rushed toward the glistening north wall. Sure enough there it was. The moonstones were oval-like pillars with iridescent white flowers growing at their base. He popped open the metal top of the glass, but stopped short.

Was it okay to touch the flower? Was it the petal or the leaf that I needed to bring back? How much am I to gather? The vial seemed small. He compared it to the petal of one of the moonstone flowers and the ampoule was only half the length of the petal. *Should I roll the petal?*

"Fool, you are wasting time." Padrick appeared next to him and grabbed at the vial. Traian, not wanting to lose it again, dodged his attempt by shifting it away. "Very well, you hold the vial and I'll put the plant inside." Padrick reached into the black soil and dug until he found a cream-colored root of one of the plants. He gave the base of the stem a good yank and came up with an entire plant. "You will need the whole thing. If this has happened once, it will happen again."

How was the elf going to put a plant the length his forearm into a small vial the size of his index finger? *This is an elf and I'm in the Otherworld.* He held the vial forward at arm's length and braced himself for what might come. Padrick placed the plant over the open vial, whispered a series of hasty words, and then let go of the plant. Traian resisted the urge to catch the falling object and tightened his grip on the vial. The moment the root end touched the side of glass, the plant shrank into the vial with a pop.

Padrick repeated the same process with a couple of moonstones the size of his palm, which turned into tiny grains of sand inside the ampoule. Traian watched in awe. The sound of large flapping wings and a gust of wind drew his attention to the center of the garden. A white, winged horse landed behind them in the clearing. Traian capped the glass and put the chain around his neck again, tucking the vial inside his tunic.

"Come." Padrick hurried toward the horse. Traian reluctantly followed.

He'd ridden a dragon, climbed a mountain, entered the Otherworld, succumbed to elven magic, had been taken captive by elves, met the elven king, snuck off with another elf, had the king's guard chase him, found what he had come for, and now a flying horse? Traian didn't know how much more magic he could take, but he still needed to get out of this land.

"This is Belanor. He will take you home. You must leave now. I will hold back the guards as long as I can." Padrick reached up and patted the horse's mane. "Hello, friend."

"Why are you helping?" Traian asked without moving closer to the horse.

Padrick turned toward him, answering in a low voice. "I'm not helping you. I'm helping *her*. Now go, before you get detained here forever, and I lose the last woman I loved."

While Traian tried to wrap his head around the new information, Belanor lowered his head and upper body so

Traian could mount him. "I have never ridden a winged horse," he said as he approached.

"Hold on to his mane and let him do the rest." Padrick held his hand where Traian could use it to hoist himself on the tallest horse he'd ever attempted to ride. "One more thing," the elf said as Traian attempted to settle onto Belanor's back, "you'll need this." Padrick held out Traian's hunting knife.

Traian didn't hesitate to take back what belonged to him. "Thank you."

"Keep your guard up," Padrick reminded him, tapping his temple.

Before any more words could be exchanged, Belanor took flight, spreading his massive feathered wings. Within a breath, they were above the trees, heading toward the mountains. As they ascended, Traian glanced down and caught one last glimpse of Padrick, the elf who had once loved the same woman he loved. Heat boiled in his throat, rising to his face. Perhaps, that was why Evelina had held back from him. Her heart was already taken.

Obviously, they weren't together anymore, but knowing there was someone of Evelina's kind, someone more powerful, who carried a torch for her only added more confusion to his situation. Until now, he hadn't considered he had any competition for Evelina's affections, but an elf? This changed the entire story. Why would she want a mere human, when there was someone who commanded flying horses and wielded magic? Though this knowledge angered Traian, it didn't change his mission or resolve.

He surveyed the land as they flew the portal to his home. More horns sounded in the distance, and he caught sight of the elves on the ground running towards the mountain they were headed. His escape wouldn't be as easy as he'd hoped.

"Faster, Belanor," he urged the horse, digging in his heels.

Traian glanced behind and noted four black flying horses closing in on them fast. Before he could think of what to do, Belanor dove to the right, as an arrow narrowly missed Traian's shoulder. The horse maneuvered again to the left barely missing the arrows shooting into the sky from the trees below.

Traian was certain they would die. Hundreds of elves moved across the forest floor. He'd succumbed to their sleepy spell too easily. He knew they had far more powerful magic. "We have to get higher, Belanor," he shouted.

The horse gained altitude quickly. Soon they were hidden within the clouds, yet he could hear the others gaining on them. At least they were safe from the arrows for now. A moment later, the clouds parted and the mountain and portal stood right in front of them. He and Belanor were going too fast. Traian was certain they would crash into the mountain. They couldn't possibly fit through the modest entrance of the portal. He braced himself for the impact.

Chapter 5

Traian closed his eyes at the last moment. Instead of getting smashed into the hard rock, he felt a loud rush of wind and then cold. He opened his eyes and they were soaring through clouds in the snowy mountains he recognized. They had made it!

His relief was short-lived as frigid air set in. *Evelina.* Was she alive? He lowered his mental shield for the first time since the elven palace and reached out with his mind towards the cave. He waited. Nothing.

Worry not, Hunter, a calm male voice echoed through his mind. He almost let go of Belanor's mane at its sound. *Please, hold on.*

"Is that you?" Traian asked, tightening his grip.

Belanor let out a neigh in response.

"You can get into people's minds too?"

No, Belanor replied. *I'm simply communicating with you. I cannot read your mind, but I can read your aura like all other animals.*

They flew through the clouds silently for a few moments before Traian responded. "Do you know where we're going?"

Yes. Padrick instructed me to follow the dragon scent, which would have been difficult as I have not smelled a dragon in my lifetime, but I recognized elven scent and the dragon accompanies her.

"Are you frightened?"

Should I be?

"No, Zara won't hurt you," Traian assured the horse, uncertain of his own words. "I'll take care of it."

Traian focused his mind again towards Evelina, but this time including Zara. *We're coming.*

Good, came the dragon's thunderous reply. He welcomed her roaring voice with relief.

As Belanor descended from the clouds, the base of the mountains appeared, then the woods, and finally the village. He longed to return to the routine they'd established. He wanted to go back to the new normal, but how could he after what he'd experienced and learned during the last few hours. That was when he noticed it or the lack thereof.

The magic fence. It wasn't there. The sense of urgency screamed from inside every cell of his body. A new wave of adrenaline filled his veins.

"Quickly." Traian sucked in his panic.

I'm going as fast as I can.

"I know," Traian patted the horse's neck with one hand and held on with the other. "The cave is to the left."

Belanor glided down to the hidden slit in the mountain as if he'd come here every day and landed at the cave entrance. Without a single pause, he galloped into the cave and leapt down to the bottom of the main cavern. Traian didn't even have to instruct the pegasus where to go as he turned towards the large tunnel entrance at the opposite side of the cavern.

They entered the cavern with the underground lake. Out on the center, Evelina floated in the glass casket with Zara standing guard. Zara released a puff of smoke as they entered the room but never shifted her gaze away from her companion. Traian almost didn't recognize her. Zara's scales had taken a brownish tint like that of a dying tree. He gave Belanor a pat on his neck and jumped down from his back, sloshing through the water to Evelina and Zara. Relief flooded his heart as he reunited with them, even though he knew they weren't clear of the curse yet.

"I have it." He held the vial hanging from his neck out.

Zara gave him a fleeting glance and returned her gaze to Evelina. "You must plant the flower first," she said in a soft roar.

Traian stopped on the opposite side of Evelina's glass cocoon. "Where?"

"Plant it on the bank of the lake, over there." Zara pointed a wing hook behind to a spot near where Belanor stood.

Traian went to that location. When he reached the place, he took off the chain from around his neck and stared at the micro plant inside the vial, unsure how to proceed. He didn't possess the magic of the elf who had put the plant inside nor speak their language. He didn't have their power. He did know that if he did not do something soon, his two closest friends would die. Traian might still hold a grudge towards Evelina, but never wished death for her or Zara.

Drop the vial onto the rock. Belanor nudged him with his nose. *I used to tend the Temple Garden as a young colt.*

He held the vial to his face and stared at the moonstone flower. The petals began to glow. Light spread throughout its leaves until everything inside the vial shone brightly like a white flame. His palm tingled. He knew where the light had come from. He might not have the magic of elves, but he had his own magic. He hoped it would be enough.

Traian placed the ampoule on the flat rock and knelt next to it. He covered the glass with both hands, feeling the tingling now. This was a new sensation. Even though he never lifted his other hand to check, he knew the white flame came from both hands. He felt the energy swirling and pulsing between his palms. As the power grew he parted his hands slowly. Through squinted eyes he watched as the bright sphere of light expanded before him. His ears popped as the energy from his hands increased in intensity.

Months ago, he would have argued that attempting to grow a plant in a rock would not provide results. Now what he thought normal had long gone out the window along with any skepticism about magic.

A small crack of glass echoed through the cavern. The sphere grew to the size of one of the milk jugs in Evelina's kitchen. Then the light dissipated, revealing the full-grown plant Padrick had held just hours before in the temple garden. The moonstones he'd included with the plant grew too and formed a small wall around the plant. The flower's petals glowed in the dimly lit cavern.

Exhaustion seized his body and he swayed. Just as he collapsed, a white nose caught him by the side.

Easy, Hunter, you've expended too much energy.

Bucking mules, the horse was right. The last time he'd rested was when he first arrived in Transpatia. So much had happened before and afterwards. Yet none of the physical or mental exertion he'd extended had crippled him like planting this moonstone flower. His arms hung lifelessly from his slouched shoulders. He still had to get the flower petals to Evelina, but he couldn't find the energy to speak. He opened his mind to Zara, knowing she would understand what needed to be done.

Well done, Hunter. I will bring her to you. Zara's voice roared through his head and he instantly sat up.

"Thank you, Belanor," he said with a weak voice as they watched Zara guide the glass cocoon toward them.

Anytime, my friend. The gentle words soothed his tired heart and strengthened his aching muscles.

With renewed energy, he turned towards the transparent cocoon. Before he could ask how to get Evelina out, the glass shattered in thousands of tiny diamond-shaped shards and vanished. He pulled Evelina into his lap with her head resting against his chest. He paused for a moment and inhaled her scent. Panic surged through every nerve of his body. Instead of sniffing her usual herbal and floral aroma, he smelled death. If he didn't get a moonstone petal in her now, she would die here in his arms.

With one hand, he plucked a single petal from the flower. He opened her mouth with the other hand and thrust it inside. When he reached for another petal, Belanor blocked his arm.

One petal is enough.

"If this is true, then why did Padrick have me take the entire plant?" Traian asked.

Belanor bowed his head. *I do not know the prince's wishes.*

"Prince? Padrick is an elven prince?"

Belanor nodded.

Traian looked down at Evelina. "Are you sure we don't need more?"

"The pegasus is correct." Zara spoke. "We must wait now."

If there was anything Traian knew well… it was waiting. He'd spent most of his hunting expeditions biding his time for the right prey to cross his path. Belanor rested behind him and he leaned back against the horse. Traian stroked Evelina's head as he watched for any sign of life and hoped he wasn't too late. Belanor loosely wrapped a wing around them, tucking Traian and Evelina into a safe embrace. Zara crouched a few paces away. She looked so lonely.

Thank you, Zara, for watching over her while I was gone.

She's all I have, Zara replied.

I know. Thank you for trusting me.

Zara snorted, releasing a puff of smoke. *Don't get cocky,*

son. If I could have avoided being slain the moment I entered Transpatia, I would have gotten the moonstone flower myself.

Traian placed his hand on top of Evelina's head and breathed deeply. The smell of death remained, but another scent stirred within the notes. He exhaled.

Evelina's eyelashes fluttered. Her green eyes stared up at him. A sigh of relief escaped his lips as he clutched her tight to his chest.

"Where are we?" Evelina murmured in a weak voice.

At first, he was surprised. How could she not know where they were? Then he realized they were surrounded by Belanor's white wing.

"Evelina, meet Belanor."

The horse lowered his wing enough so she could see his head, and he neighed. Evelina's eyes grew large.

"How did he get here?" she asked as she shifted her eyes back to Traian.

Before he could answer her question, Zara bounded over to get a glimpse of her companion. A faint smile spread across Evelina's lips. Without hesitation, Belanor lowered his wing to let Zara join their little circle. Zara gave Evelina a gentle nudge with her nose. A low rumble of content filled the cavern. Evelina sighed and closed her eyes accepting the great beast's affection.

I understand now. Traian knew what Belanor meant. He remembered the first time he'd witnessed the intimate connection his mentor and her dragon shared. No human words could describe their bond. One could not exist without the other. He noticed some of Zara's scales. They glowed bright red again. Had Belanor not reached them in time, there would have been two deaths and the village people would have been next.

"The barrier..." Traian said.

Zara threw her head back and roared. "She is too weak, as am I. We need a few hours to regain our strength."

Perhaps I can help? The moment Belanor spoke, Evelina's eyes opened and looked at the horse. Zara stared at him too. They all had "heard" him.

"Of course, you can." Evelina attempted to sit up but slumped against Traian's chest, defeated. She focused on him. "You must go with the horse. I will channel the spell through him and you can guide him around the perimeter of the village."

"Won't people see us?" Traian asked.

No, Belanor replied. *I can disguise us from the human eye.*

"Traian, you must go now," Evelina urged.

Seeing her so weak pained him. He knew she would be safe with Zara in the cave. The moonstone would continue to work on her enfeebled body and in a matter of time she would regain her strength.

"Very well," Traian agreed. He laid Evelina on the cool ground and checked around for something to cover her.

"Stop wasting time," Zara roared, "and go save the village. Be careful, for I feel evil tarries nigh."

Traian kissed Evelina's forehead. "I will be back."

"You'd better," she whispered.

Traian jumped onto Belanor's back with ease, though this was only his second ride. Belanor galloped through the cavern and tunnel before taking flight through the exit. A breath later, they broke through the top of the mountain into the sky, Traian shaded his eyes while they adjusted to the intense light. As soon as he could see again, he gasped. The barrier was completely gone. A few sparks flashed on the forest floor and the last of the magical shield vanished.

Where do we begin?

Traian nudged Belanor to the south of the valley. Belanor's great wings pounded the air as they hovered at the entrance to the valley. For a few moments, nothing happened. Then a few white sparks appeared on the ground. With each flap of Belanor's mighty wings, more and more sparks appeared, creating a wall. As the light climbed higher they moved towards the center of the village. Traian felt his hands glow again. He let go of Belanor's mane and spread his arms out. A veil of white sparks poured from his palms and joined the sparks below. The sphere of light spread across the valley until they reached the northern mountains.

They stopped and turned to examine their work. A dome of shimmering white light protected the entire valley and the surrounding mountains. Satisfaction spread through his body as he lowered his arms. Traian's body felt weak from the magic, but he didn't care. He'd traveled into Transpatia and back, and had planted a moonstone plant. Evelina was alive, his adopted people were safe again, and he had a new glorious pegasus for a friend. All in a day's work.

The sense of accomplishment lasted only for half a breath. A dark object moved on the southern horizon. The distance was too great for him to see clearly, but he knew it was alive. The creature spread its wings and disappeared behind the mountains. He could feel the malicious energy flowing in its wake. There was only one thing to do.

Something red entered in Traian's periphery. Zara stood on the perch near her entrance to the mountain. They made eye contact.

Do not go after him, Hunter. Her words sliced through his mind. *You are not ready.*

Zara was right. He didn't have the strength to battle

anything. He barely had enough strength to sit on Belanor. As if hearing his thoughts, Belanor turned toward the mountain. When he landed next to the dragon, Evelina emerged from the rock slit and joined them.

"Marvelous." She threw her arms around his neck as he dismounted the winged horse. "I knew you could do it."

Traian welcomed her embrace, but could barely stand. He leaned against Belanor and wrapped one arm around Evelina while the other held Belanor's mane. He quickly realized that instead of him holding her up she held him. *How had she regained her strength so quickly?* Energy poured off her, filling and fortifying his muscles.

"How?" Traian asked.

Evelina smiled at him and squeezed his waist with her arms. "You. All of it." He stared blankly. She continued, "You used your power. Belanor amplified it with his, and channeled my protection spell. Because you took the burden of the magic, my body recovered quickly." Her stomach gave a loud rumble. "And I'm hungry." She laughed.

He chuckled, but then his stomach growled in agreement, as did Belanor's and Zara's. Each of them had worked hard today. While staying alive and traveling between worlds, food had been the last thing on anyone's mind.

"I need to hunt," Zara said. "You children behave while

I'm gone." She leapt from the cliff ledge and headed south.
Traian could only speculate where she was going to hunt.

Belanor neighed. *I spotted a patch of fresh spring grass in a
meadow below, which is perfect for me to regain my strength.* The
winged horse jumped off the edge of the cliff and swooped
down into the valley, disappearing behind the trees in the
east.

A cool, spring wind blew around them. The sun had
disappeared behind the western mountain at their back.
Evening hour hung in the air. Evelina took Traian's hand and
led him down to the entrance into the mountain. But before
they stepped into the darkness, she whirled around and
placed a hand on his chest.

"I never said thank you," she whispered.

He said nothing, but nodded his head.

"You saved us. And I'm sure you have many
questions." She lowered her gaze. "You know the truth now
and I understand if you do not trust me anymore."

All the emotions Traian had kept buried until now
came bubbling up like an artesian mountain spring. He
expected the anger and betrayal to taste bitter on his tongue,
but it didn't. Yes, he wasn't pleased with the revelations of his
trip to the Otherworld, yet he couldn't be angry with her now
that she was awake and breathing. He wanted to rage about

how she'd withheld valuable information, but he simply didn't have the energy or will to do so. He'd nearly lost her, the guardian of his people, the woman of his heart. There would be time to discuss and argue all the complications of his journey, her secret, and what should be done about the simmering evil in the southern horizon. Right now, there was only one thing far more important he wanted to do, and he didn't waste any time.

Cupping her face with one hand, Traian drew her to him with the other around her waist. He tilted her chin and kissed her soft, rosy lips, leaning into the kiss enjoying all the tingling and warmth radiating through his body. He moved in closer, kissed her harder. Something seemed off. His vision darkened. Her lips cooled and hardened. He blinked and Evelina disappeared. In her place stood a cold, solid rock.

Chapter 6

Traian blinked. He was in the cave, alone. Evelina, Zara, and Belanor no longer walked the earth. He laid his cheek on the cold, rock surface and wept, staining the cave floor with crimson tears. Even though dozens of centuries had passed, this was the first time he'd allowed himself to cry and feel the excruciating pain of his loss. Why did he keep going? His existence wasn't living. The joy of life had gone long ago when the love of his life had taken her last breath. He longed to walk through the portal into Transpatia and meet his end by elven arrows, but that escape route had been sealed ages ago.

The answer did not lie with the elves but with the vampires. No matter what he did, he could not be put down. Tortured, yes, but executed, no. His master enjoyed watching him suffer too much. His pain was his master's pleasure. That is why he still existed.

Oh, look at yourself! he scolded and stood up. *Enough wallowing.* He wiped all the tears with a handkerchief then tucked the blood-soaked cloth back in his coat pocket.

Above him, a familiar voice chuckled, "It's about time you pulled yourself together."

The sound of that voice was enough to send Traian into a rage. A split second later, his wings were out and he launched to the ledge where Padrick crouched. Before the elf could move, Traian had him on his back. With fangs out, Traian was ready to shred the elf's throat.

"Easy, man, I'm here to help." Padrick flashed a white smile. "Elven promise."

"You threw that rock at me, didn't you?" Traian spat in his face. "Tell me why I shouldn't kill you now?"

"Because." Padrick wiped the red drops from his brow. "I am here to help you bring her back."

"What?" Traian jerked his head away.

"It's the vernal full moon on the equinox with a planetary alignment."

The words rang in Traian's head. He'd heard this before. It sounded like something Satra would say, as she was always spewing forth prophecies. He ignored most of them. Maybe he should have paid more attention. He released Padrick and stood up.

"How?"

"Oh, my friend." Padrick brushed himself and stood

up. "It's quite simple. We must find the moonstone and call her spirit." He walked to the end of the tunnel leading outside.

"We are not friends, nor will we ever be." Traian said, following him. When they exited the mountain, they were met by silver moonlight. "How do we find the moonstone?"

Padrick laughed. "Already ahead of you, bro." He raised his hand and revealed a flat, oblong moonstone. "Did a little exploring while I waited for you to wake up. Sorry about that, by the way. Shall we?"

Traian really would have ripped out his smooth, white throat then and there, but the elf had power and could probably do what he said. As much as he hated him, Padrick held the keys to realms he could no longer access as a strigoi.

"We shall," Traian said and grabbed his arm, "but you must promise me this. If we do not succeed in bringing her back, you must finish me."

"With pleasure, brother," Padrick agreed with a snide grin. Traian released the elf's arm.

Padrick set the milky white stone on the ground between them and pulled a knife from his leather boot. With one quick slice of his palm he squeezed several juicy drops of blood. He handed Traian the knife. "Your turn."

"I can't do anything, remember?" Traian shook his

head.

"You still have your soul, bloodsucker." Padrick hissed. "You can call her because you are connected."

"I have tried. It doesn't work." Traian gritted his teeth.

"Stupid, pig-headed fiend. It's the *vernal moon*. It didn't work before because the time wasn't right and you needed me, of course."

Traian thought about that for a moment. He knew the elf had ulterior motives, because elves always did. But why the hell not try? He took the knife and copied what the elf had done, adding his dark, undead blood to the elf's vibrant, pink onto the stone. The air shifted around them the moment they combined. Padrick stood and closed his eyes. As he raised his arms, he turned to face the moon.

"Blood of elf, blood of your soulmate, we call upon the one taken away too soon. Your time has come. Return to this realm and walk among us once more. Hear my call, oh daughter of the elven king, spinner of magic, and lover of life."

The mountain shook and groaned. Traian held the side of the cliff to steady himself. He glanced down at the blood. It glowed brighter and brighter, until it was too painful to look at. Rocks from higher up the ridge tumbled down the side of the mountain around them. Padrick stood in the same spot, unmoved. The ruckus ended as fast as it had started. When Traian stared down at the stone, it had cracked into a thousand pieces. Their blood had vanished.

Padrick opened his eyes and smiled. "It is done. Her spirit has been released. She will be reborn, but, alas, in human form."

"That's it?" Traian released his hold on the cliff and walked over to the remnants of the moonstone.

"What did you expect?"

Traian shook his head and picked up a speck of the moonstone. Just then a mighty gust of wind blew the rest of the pieces down the mountain. He put the speck into his breast coat pocket. "And now we wait."

"And now we wait." Padrick repeated and jumped down to a lower cliff perch. "We shall cross paths again." He disappeared into the shadow of the valley below. Traian had no doubt he would see the elf again. Could the little magic he'd witnessed have worked? He'd waited four thousand years for Evelina. He would wait for another four thousand if needed. Until then, there was much work to be done. He turned and disappeared back into the mountain.

To be continued…

Mating Dance

A Legends of Carpatia Tale

This story is dedicated to those who've found their soulmates
and
those who are still searching.

Chapter 1

Traian stood at the entrance of the cave watching his strigoi coven moving possessions into their new home. Since finding the ancient lair last spring, he'd been spending all his waking hours modifying the place to include modern comforts such as electricity, electronic communication, refrigerators, appliances, hot tubs, and security systems. His small coven helped as much as they could, though they didn't share his passion and enthusiasm for the place. Justina, his second in command, voiced her opinions the loudest. Traian never had to remind her he was her master since he'd turned her centuries ago until last month.

He couldn't blame the other coven members. They didn't understand the value of this place like he did. The group was literally sitting on an ancient place where powerful magic once flowed. Though strigoi, as vampires were called in their country of Romania, did not possess magical talents like humans or otherworldly creatures, they made up for it in other ways. Many had the strength to haul tons of equipment up the side of a remote mountain without physically tiring. Mental fatigue was another matter.

Traian watched them carry in the last of the furniture. Cornel trudged near the back of the group with his massive coffin. Traian followed him into the cave, closing the meter-thick steel door behind him. They continued through the lit tunnels into the mountain to the main cavern where he'd made significant changes. He'd cleared all the centuries-old rubble and created a central space for everyone to train, socialize, rest, and entertain. The ancient coves around the main cave had been carved deeper in the natural rock, and he'd used the loose stones to create walls. These areas became rooms for the coven and their servants. His room was away from the others deeper into the mountain near the underground lake cave. He preferred this arrangement.

Traian glanced up to a crevice in the rock, where he'd watched a great, red dragon come and go long before any of his coven were a speck in their parents' eyes. Nostalgia formed a lump in his throat. They were here, finally.

"Justina, check the security system and verify we are online," Traian commanded, "Cornel, please check the gate, and double-check that it's secure." He pointed to the slit above them. "I will be in my quarters."

His subjects nodded, and Traian headed into the tunnel

leading to his chamber. He longed for peace and quiet and needed a moment to allow emotions to pass in solitude and without an audience.

Traian's room held few possessions. After existing for more than four thousand years, he had lost all desire for *belongings*. Located in the back corner, his coffin was positioned for sleeping in during the dark phase of the moon. All strigoi did. In the opposite corner, stood a chair with a cello on a stand. Strigoi didn't *sleep* much; therefore, finding things to occupy their minds during waking hours was sometimes difficult. Each coven member had his or her own way of dealing with this by choosing various subjects for studying or learning a new language or playing an instrument. At the entrance wall, a desk displayed the newest model of a personal computer. On the other side of the desk, a closet contained several coats like the one he wore, an extra pair of boots, and his silver knives.

While his coven used guns now for defense, he preferred knives and arrows. Traian had retired quiver and bow centuries ago, but knives had become part of his body. Even when he bathed, he kept them close. After a thousand years of being tortured with silver, the metal didn't bother his skin as younger strigoi.

The vampire walked over to the desk and sat down.

From his breast pocket, he pulled out the speck of moonstone and rolled the tiny crystal between his thumb and finger, recalling the spell Padrick had done and all that had happened before. His memory drifted further into the distant past, back to the days when his heart beat. In those days, he sat outside of the cave as he had done earlier this night. Just like that, he was back in the moment.

Chapter 2

Evelina hurried out of the cave entrance carrying a basket covered with a linen cloth. A cloak flowed from her shoulders in a cobalt wave. The white elven dress beneath the blue mantle glowed in the summer sunlight against the green grass at her feet. Traian's heart raced as it always did when he saw her. Since the close call three moons before, he'd moved into the cave with her, Zara, and Belanor, his winged-horse friend. The four of them had taken every precaution to keep the village safe. Each took watches both day and night keeping an eye on the valley and its surrounding mountains. No sightings of dark creatures since Traian returned from Transpatia. The village hadn't had new visitors either, which caused a bit of concern among the people.

This could only mean two things; no one was alive beyond their valley or people didn't travel anymore due to illness and war. Either case didn't inspire confidence in their safety. Many settlements to the south and north had fallen victim, so Traian and Evelina began training the young village men in the ways of battle. The Northern Tribes had not been seen in more than a year, but the Southern Savages continued to wreak havoc through those lands. None, however, had been seen near Carpatia Valley since Evelina's poisoning.

Today, he and Evelina would take a break from training and enjoy a quiet meal in the meadow on the north side of the valley. He'd wanted to take Evelina there since he found the location on one of his hunts. She'd agreed to his invitation this morning. Belanor even offered to fly them there before he relieved Zara from her watch. Evelina had packed the food. Now that they possessed the moonstone flower from Traian's excursion into Transpatia, Evelina had made a tincture to ensure the food or drink they consumed was safe.

Traian watched Evelina as she fiddled with the basket covering and then with her cloak. She'd never appeared this restless before. "What is wrong?" he asked.

"Oh, nothing, I want everything to be perfect. You know me." Evelina let out an anxious giggle.

Why was she nervous? Traian wondered. "Let me take that." He reached for the basket.

"No, I can manage." She pulled away from him.

Very strange. Traian mulled over her odd behavior. Maybe she didn't want to be alone with him. Since he'd moved into the cavern, Traian hadn't had a waking moment unaccompanied with Evelina. Either Belanor or Zara had been there with them, or they were down in the village training the handful of warriors. Even though they slept in the same room, at least ten steps separated their beds, something Traian didn't like... but accepted. They rarely had a moment to themselves, let alone with each other. But what bothered him the most is the distance she kept between them. If they touched during training she would break contact as quickly as possible.

Belanor landed on a ledge near them. *Ready?* the pegasus asked. The steed's smooth voiced filled Traian's mind.

Traian nodded. He let Evelina lead the way and mount the horse before he settled behind her. She scooted forward just enough that their bodies wouldn't touch.

Pain sliced at Traian's heart. *Why was she acting like this?* Sure, they weren't lovers, but he'd proven to Evelina the lengths he would go to protect her. Why didn't she trust him? Traian had heard one answer but chose to ignore. He refused to believe the difference in their races mattered. He knew Evelina fancied him. She'd responded to his show of affection on previous occasions, but always pulled away before passions overcame them both. He tried not to be bitter, but this time he couldn't.

Before Traian could stuff these unresting thoughts, Belanor launched into the air raising his front legs high enough to cause Evelina to slide into Traian's chest. He wrapped an arm around her waist and held onto Belanor's mane with the other.

Thank you, mate. He channeled the thought to his companion, something he'd mastered only last week.

My pleasure.

Evelina stiffened at the closeness, but relaxed into Traian mid-flight. Belanor sliced the travel time to the meadow in half, but Traian cherished this nearness to the elf who'd stolen his heart no matter how quickly it was over.

When Belanor landed, Evelina jumped off immediately. "This place is lovely. I had forgotten the beauty here," she said and hurried to the center of the meadow.

To Traian, Evelina didn't seem like someone enjoying the scenery, but acted as if she'd been thrust into this situation even though she'd accepted his invitation.

"We don't have to do this, you know," he said without dismounting. "You can get back on, and we can go home... if you'd rather."

"No, no, I want this very much." Evelina walked in a circle, then stopped. "Ah-ha, perfect place for a meal. I shall set up right away." She knelt and started unloading the basket in her hand.

Traian hesitated a breath longer before jumping down. "Thank you, friend. We'll see you in a while." He patted Belanor's neck.

She'll come around. Be patient. Belanor neighed and leapt into the sky.

Traian watched his friend disappear past the trees. Even though Belanor was gone, Traian still felt his connection, something that had taken some getting used to, but he didn't mind. Traian turned toward Evelina, but didn't know what to say or do. Evelina bustled about setting bundles of food on the linen cloth she'd spread on the grass. Traian checked around for something to busy himself with but found nothing to occupy his time. He spotted a patch of blue flowers a few steps away from their picnic area and meandered there, plucking a handful of blossoms. He'd seen his sisters do that when they were young girls. Traian tied the flowers together with a blade of grass.

Birds chirped in the trees surrounding the open area. A gentle breeze rustled the foliage below. Sunlight filled the meadow, bathing everything in summer warmth. Traian took a deep breath and filled his lungs with the refreshing air of the living forest, a stark contrast to the confining space of the cave. He missed waking up to the choir of nature outside the window of his thatched-roofed burdei. Traian's life had changed much in one year. His life before taking shelter in this valley seemed like an old nightmare.

"It's ready," Evelina called.

Traian waited a moment before responding, not wanting Evelina to think him too eager. He kept the flowers behind his back, unsure if she would like them or consider the nosegay a childish gesture.

He knelt on the cloth across from her and waited. Evelina glanced up at him and smiled before her gaze dropped to the open bundles of food. Traian lowered his focus to them too, and his stomach growled in delight. Dried fruit, fresh greens from the village garden, nuts, cheese, and fresh bread. A jug of wine sat between them. Breaking bread with Evelina was one of the few pleasures he looked forward to. Today was better because they were alone.

"Eat." Evelina gestured toward the food. "I know you are hungry."

Traian took a deep breath. "Before we start, can we talk?"

Evelina placed both hands in her lap and looked up. "Okay, get it out before I burst into a thousand pieces." Her words didn't match the body stance, but Traian knew elves had mastered the appearance of calm long before humans had settled into this valley.

Before he could say anything, Evelina launched right in. "I'm the king's daughter… firstborn and the rightful heir to the throne of Transpatia."

Traian's jaw dropped. This was not what he'd expected for her to say.

Evelina held a hand up. "I'm not finished. Please, let me say everything I've been holding in." Traian rolled his wrist for her to continue.

"Long ago before I was born, there was a war between the dragons and elves. The elves won and drove out all the dragons from Transpatia. My ancestors broke all the eggs and burned the beasts' nests. They hunted the dragons into this world until they were certain all had been destroyed. If anyone found remaining eggs, they were to be destroyed. Harboring dragon eggs has always been punishable by death. I was told dragons were pure evil and were considered part demon. During warrior survival training, I was dropped into an unknown territory and had to fend for myself for a complete lunar cycle…"

The longer Evelina spoke, more questions filled Traian's mind, distracting him from her actual words. *Why had she waited this long to reveal critical information to him?* Evelina stood and started her usual pacing as she continued sharing new info.

"…and I couldn't help it. She stared up at me. We bonded. I couldn't kill her nor could I allow anyone else to save her. Under cover of night, I snuck her out of our world and into this one. To my regret, I hadn't been sneaky enough. Even though my father's guards didn't find her, they knew of my travels. After I had finished my training, I continued to come to this side of the portal to feed Zara. As she grew, it was harder to conceal her in the cave, and she needed to eat more than I could provide."

Traian cocked his head to one side and tried hard to concentrate on her words.

"I had to teach her how to hunt. We spent most nights together. I couldn't be away too long because we needed to be near each other to rebuild our strength. My father had become concerned with my constant travel, and I knew if he found out the truth, he would have sent one hundred sentinels to kill her. When asked, I lied and told him I loved the humans and wanted to live here. My father gave me two choices: come home and continue my training to become the future queen, or stay here forever with the humans and forfeit my crown. If I chose this world, I could never go home again, and if I picked Transpatia, I could never return here until I became queen."

Traian watched her brows furrow as she dug the heel of her foot into the grass.

Evelina paused for a moment, "You know my answer. I really had only one choice. And now you know who I am and why I am here." She looked up at him. "Are you ever going to give me those flowers behind your back?"

Traian's head reeled with all the new information Evelina had shared. He'd forgotten about the flowers, but he held them out, and she took the small bouquet, raising the blue blossoms to her nose.

"Why didn't you tell me this before?" Traian asked.

"Isn't it obvious?" Evelina threw her hands in the air. A few loose petals glided down to her feet. "I'm an elf in a human land."

"So?"

"I could be hunted for my blood."

"Humans hunt you?" he scoffed. "No one knows you exist."

"Not living humans, but the undead. My blood gives them power. Why do you think my father wants nothing to do with this world?" Evelina bowed and answered her own question. "He doesn't want to risk his people's lives."

Traian nodded in understanding. "Okay, but that still doesn't justify why you didn't tell *me* before."

Evelina straightened and sighed. Traian watched her red face turn into the emotionless, pale mask she usually wore. "Maybe my father was right. Humans will never understand us." Evelina turned her back to him.

That was it. Traian couldn't take another of her stoic displays. "Oh, bloody, hoof-headed woman. How could any of us understand because you never give us a chance?" Traian sprung to his feet. "What does a man have to do? I traveled into your land without a smidgen of knowledge of your kind to save your pretty, little behind. Every day, I work hard by your side to help these people have a better chance to defend themselves against an evil we don't quite understand. Every night, I sleep near you while honoring your space. I stand quietly and let you take the lead in everything. What do I have to do to prove my loyalty?"

Evelina cast a curious glance at him over her shoulder.

"It ends now. I need to know why you keep me at a distance when we are together and still share much of our lives?" He sliced the air with his hand. "If you do not want me, please say so."

Halfway through Traian's rant, Evelina had turned to face him. Her eyes widened. He'd only seen that a few times since he'd known her. One time was when Traian had held the light on that special winter night. Evelina eyed him in another way now, the indifferent façade cracked as her mouth dropped. She moved her lips as if to say something, but seemed unable to get the words out.

"You?" Evelina swallowed and shook her head. "You think I don't care?

"Well, you haven't given me any evidence to the contrary." Traian crossed his arms over his chest.

Evelina mimicked his position. "Why do you think I had you move into the cave and let you sleep in my quarters?"

"What does that have to do with anything? *Nothing* is happening." Traian couldn't believe her nerve.

"It's complicated."

"Somehow I doubt it."

Evelina's face turned red again. This was the most emotion Traian had seen from her other than when he'd kissed her rosy lips. Evelina's reactions greatly entertained him, but Traian had shielded his mind this morning when she'd stepped out of the cave before coming to the meadow. Most of the time, Traian let his mind open to her, although it angered him that he even had to voice his thoughts. Surely, she'd read them long before.

Evelina circled around the cloth on the ground with the forgotten food until she stood directly in front of him. She reached for one of his flexed arms and closed her eyes. He loved it when Evelina touched him, but this was different, more like a caress one would give a domesticated beast of burden, not a confidant or lover. Traian stepped back, breaking contact with her.

"Please," Evelina pleaded as she reached out again. He took one long stride back. She lowered her hand. "I understand what you feel, but you can't. I am sorry I have given you the wrong impression."

"You lie."

Evelina shook her head. "It's the truth. Humans and elves cannot mate or intermingle. It's forbidden."

"By who?"

"The elven laws."

"But you" — Traian jabbed his finger in her direction — "just told me you chose this world, not yours. Therefore, you are free of those rules."

The color vanished from Evelina's face, and she cast her gaze away from him. "Not this rule."

"Mule cakes, I don't believe you."

"I could snap your neck in the furrows of passion. You've seen my strength, and I always hold back." Evelina folded her hands behind her. "That isn't the real reason. The meddling of species is forbidden on all plains and worlds. That is how evil is born."

He was about to say something when, without warning, a gray pegasus landed next to them. On the back of the winged horse sat Padrick.

Chapter 3

"Greetings." Padrick flashed a grin. Traian had never seen him smile before. "Did I interrupt something?"

Multiple ways to mutilate that pretty face flashed through Traian's mind as his hands balled into fists. He'd wondered when he'd see the elf again, but not today. Traian glanced at Evelina. She had her expressionless mask back on and stood tall, chin lifted high, shoulders squared.

Padrick jumped off the winged steed. His smile vanished with one glance at the former elven princess. Though Traian couldn't hear their thoughts, he knew a conversation was happening between the two. Padrick narrowed his eyes at her for a moment and turned to Traian. "I am being rude. I'm here to extend an invitation to Eve. By order of the king, you are to attend the Royal Midsummer Festival. By you, I mean Eve only. You, Hunter, have been forbidden to ever step foot in Transpatia again."

"As if I would want to waste my time in your horrid land," Traian mumbled.

"Why would my father want me back?" Evelina asked.

"Your brush with death has made him reconsider your banishment." Padrick turned toward the horse. "We must go now."

Traian stepped between Padrick and Evelina. "What if this is a trap?" he warned her.

Evelina shook her head. "It isn't."

Traian lowered his voice. "I don't trust him."

Evelina looked up and met Traian's gaze. She placed one hand on his cheek. "I have to go, but will be back before the festival in the village tonight." She reached up and brushed her lips against his before joining the other elf.

Padrick remounted his horse and extended a hand to Evelina, but she refused his aid, leaping onto the back and settling behind him. One hand still held the blue flowers. Padrick turned to Traian. "You have my thanks for keeping her alive."

Before Traian could respond, the horse took to the air and disappeared behind the trees. "I didn't do it for you." His answer unheard.

Traian's appetite had flown away with the elves, but an angry fire took its place. He kicked the jug of wine across the meadow. When it hit the nearest tree and shattered, he regretted his reaction. The liquid it contained could have eased the pain of his misfortune. So many revelations… so many unanswered questions… and so much unfairness. All he had wanted was a nice meal with Evelina outside in the sunshine; in turn, they'd argued, Padrick had interrupted, and now she was gone. Traian repressed the urge to call Belanor and follow the elves back to their world, but he knew he would be captured or killed the moment he stepped through the portal.

He recited Evelina's last words over and over in his mind. Would she really be back before the festival? Traian had forgotten about the upcoming celebration. These feast days didn't mean anything to him. But to Evelina, they were important points in time when magic grew strong. She would have to come back because she couldn't be separated from Zara for long. Oh, *Zara*. Did she know?

Traian broke into a run through the forest heading back to the mountain. He could have called Belanor, but he needed the physical exertion to burn off his frustration. Why would she go back to Transpatia after what she'd shared moments ago? Traian still didn't understand where Padrick stood in Evelina's life. Was he her friend, lover, or betrothed? Padrick was an elven prince. Those thoughts provided a distraction as he ran back to the cave.

Traian knew he was close when he heard Zara's roar.

She flew out from the mountain exit above him. "How could you let her go?" Tongues of crimson fire exploded from her red mouth.

"As if I could stop her," Traian shouted back.

The dragon landed next to him and stomped a front foot. She let out a growl so loud branches of nearby trees cracked and broke off.

"No magic can hide that sound." Traian covered his ears.

"We are doomed." Zara's voice echoed as a cross between a roar and wail. Her head drooped down along with her wings.

Traian lowered his arms. The last time he'd heard so much sadness and desperation in the ferocious dragon, Evelina had almost died of poisoning. "But she's in her homeland," he said.

"Pff." Zara let out a puff of smoke. "You know better than anyone that her life is in danger."

"Padrick will keep her safe." Traian didn't know why he said that, but deep in his bones he knew it to be true. Padrick had already risked much for Evelina.

"That may be, but her father rules the land. He could imprison her. Since they meddled with your mind, we can only guess what they already know." Zara shook her head.

"We are doomed."

Traian had nothing to say. They *were* probably doomed. Maybe, but he hadn't lost hope yet. "She said she'd be back before the festival tonight."

"Evelina may have said that just to appease you," Zara responded and flapped her wings. "There is no time to mope about. Much needs to be done to protect the village. I will scout the southern and northern lands to make sure no threat lurks nearby. Belanor will be close if you need anything. He can communicate with me."

"How far are you going to go?" Traian asked.

"Farther than I've gone before." Zara lowered her head and wings. She gave him a gentle nuzzle. "If we don't return, Belanor knows the protection spells to keep you and the people safe."

Traian ran a hand over the smooth, red scales on her head. "I do not like the way you speak."

"I am being realistic," Zara said. "Bringing you here was the second-best decision I ever made."

"And your first?"

"Bonding with Eve." Zara's eyes glistened. "I had hoped we'd have more time together and the two of you would realize you are made for each other."

"Worry not, dear Zara." Traian placed both hands on

either side of Zara's majestic head. "We will survive this. Evelina will come back."

"I thank you for your kind words, Hunter." Zara closed her eyes for a moment, taking in his affection. "Regardless, I must prepare for the worst. I owe that to all of you."

"You don't owe us a thing," Traian replied.

"Oh, but I do. This valley has been my home for the last fifty years." Zara lifted her head and focused up the mountain to the cliff ledge where the dragon's entrance stood. She returned her gaze to Traian. "You will have Belanor. He is a good steed and will be with you until the time comes for you to join your ancestors."

Traian leaned in and placed his lips on the spot between the dragon's nostrils for a moment. His heart broke into a million pieces at Zara's words. He had not known the depth of his love for this beast until now. "Thank you," he whispered.

The dragon purred for a breath and then stepped back. "Until we meet again," she said and leapt into the sky.

Traian watched her disappear past the tree line. He sucked in his breath thinking about the turn of events. Since all his plans had turned into a pile of fresh mule dung, Traian figured he'd move on to the next task of the day — hunting. He turned to climb the mountain to the cave entrance when

Belanor dropped out of the sky, landing behind him.

He whirled around to face his friend and breathed a sigh of relief. "Your timing is impeccable."

I am so sorry. I felt him enter our world, but I spied that same black flying creature in the south. This is the second time it has appeared so close. Belanor trotted to join Traian.

"That is the direction Zara went." He faced the south and opened his mind to the dragon. *It's back. Be careful.*

The response came immediately in a thunderous roar. *I know.*

"We should go with her." Traian turned back toward Belanor. "We can't let her deal with that thing alone."

Zara can handle herself. Belanor's smooth voice came as a calming wave. *You, however, need to get your hunting done for the festival.*

"Blast that festival. I do not care to go, but I will hunt for them."

You may be surprised. You may find pleasure if you let yourself, Belanor quipped.

Traian shook his head. "No, not with Evelina gone."

She's not the only female at the festival. Remember, this is a time to celebrate life and fertility with whomever your heart desires.

You know very well whom my heart desires. Traian channeled his thought to Belanor and broke into a run up the mountain to the entrance to the cave.

Belanor took flight the opposite direction. *I will scan the southern border. Oh, and I spotted a buck in the eastern woods.*

Chapter 4

Hours later, Traian dragged a massive buck through a newly decorated village to the butcher's hut. Flower garlands adorned every eave, post, and fence of the settlement. Tents sprouted around the center square and throughout the village. He knew very well what those were for and he knew as sure as the arrows in his quiver, he wouldn't be stepping into any of them tonight. He brushed that thought aside and heaved the buck onto the butcher's table outside the open burdei.

"Many thanks, Hunter," the rotund man with a large blade said from inside. "We sure eat well since you've come to us. May the gods bless you tonight." His belly jiggled with his laugh.

Traian nodded and stared up at the sky. The sun drew nearer the western mountains. A few more hours and the festival would be on its way. He would not be a part of it. Not without Evelina. Neither she nor Zara had made contact since Traian had last seen either of them. Even Belanor hadn't heard from Zara.

This situation concerned him. He opened his mind. *Hunting is done. We must go find Zara.*

A moment later Belanor responded. *It is too dangerous. Why don't you go bathe yourself and prepare for the festival?*

"What's the point?" he said out loud.

"What's that, son?" the butcher asked.

"Never mind." Traian waved at the man and turned toward the western mountains.

The point is Evelina promised to return tonight. You wouldn't want to greet her smelling of deer carcass and man sweat? Belanor said.

Traian hated that the horse spoke the truth. On his way out of the village, he passed his old burdei and poked his head inside the empty house. No one had moved in since he'd vacated the place. Traian missed living at the village edge close to the wilderness, but still nearby his adopted people. He missed the rich smells of burnt wood, dirt, and living forest. He missed waking up each morning to the bird chatter outside his windows. Most of all, he missed the naivety and innocence he'd enjoyed before Evelina showed him her cave where he met Zara. He often wished he hadn't learned all the things he'd discovered in the last six months. The weight of his growing knowledge threatened to crush him at times. Like today.

No time for self-pity. He needed to wash and rest because tonight could bring anything. Deep in his heart, Traian hoped Evelina would keep her word, but he didn't want to wish for something that wouldn't happen. He needed to face the reality that she probably didn't care for him as deeply. Time to move on. Although where could he go? Outside this valley were dangers beyond any human control.

But you survived just fine until last summer. The small voice of his conscience spoke. *I've become too complacent here,* Traian admitted. Until his home settlement had been destroyed by the Southern Savages, he feared nothing. Now he knew of evils that could completely wipe humans off the face of the land. Traian checked his right hand. *Light.* Within a blink of an eye, a white flame appeared in his palm.

A smile spread across Traian's face. He wasn't so helpless now — a welcome change from when he had stepped foot into this valley nearly a year before. Maybe the time had come to branch out on his own. As kind as the people of this village had been to him as a stranger, Traian never felt quite at home.

But you vowed to protect them. The same small voice spoke again.

Yeah, and look where it's gotten me? A sour taste filled his mouth. *I gave my word, and I will not take it back.*

Sure, he'd vowed to protect the people, but the promise was to Evelina and Zara. Neither of them were to be found at this moment. The elf and dragon duo were supposed to protect these people too. *But why should they now that Belanor and I are here?* The sudden realization slapped Traian like a slimy day-old dead fish. The flame in his hand extinguished at the thought.

"Fool." Traian spat on the dirt floor.

"Hunter!" A woman's voice called from outside the hut. Traian stepped out to find one of the village councilwomen dressed in a bright red dress standing by the entrance. "I apologize for disturbing you, but I'm concerned for Evelina."

Aren't we all? thought Traian, but he bowed to the councilwoman without a word.

"She wasn't at the final festival preparation gathering at noon, and none of us have seen her all day. She is supposed to initiate the opening ceremony," the councilwoman said, folding her arms across her chest. "Do you know where she is?"

"I apologize for the miscommunication. Evelina had to leave unexpectedly this morning. She said she would be here for the festival though," Traian replied in a shaky voice.

"Do you believe she will come?"

"Um...I want to believe that."

The councilwoman narrowed her eyes a Traian for a moment. "Right, well, then you will have to do the ceremony because you are the closest replacement. I'm sure she has taught you the ritual. It will break the tradition of having a woman lead, but we will live." She waved a hand and spun around. "Be at the town hall at sundown."

Before Traian could respond, the woman had disappeared around the building. He couldn't believe his continued bad luck. Traian had almost caught up to the councilwoman to tell her he'd changed his mind. Instead, he remained frozen in place.

Worry not, Hunter. Belanor's words echoed in Traian's head. *I will help you. I know the ritual and will tell you what to say and do. Meet me at the cave in an hour.*

How had Belanor heard the conversation? Traian turned to the skies, but did not see any sign of the winged horse. He growled and kicked a fence post on the way out of the village as he continued his journey to the cave. *How had he been so stupid?*

With each step up the mountain, he replayed every event since last Yule. He obviously had some magic of his own. Zara must have known that when she'd lured him into this valley with *that* buck. Evelina had trained him. Yet he didn't really progress until after her poisoning and his trip into Transpatia. Belanor had returned with him, and the winged horse had magic of his own. So why would the dragon and elf need to stay here any longer? They didn't owe these humans anything. When Traian reached the opening in the mountain, he chose to sit on the boulder next to the entrance instead of kicking it. He gripped the sides of his head with his fingertips and leaned forward.

Traian could leave now. He could grab a small bundle of possessions and leave. No one would stop him, except for Zara and Evelina, neither of which were anywhere to be found. He'd had enough of secrets and magic. He swallowed hard and stood, clenching his fists. Traian would play along for the rest of the day, but he would disappear as soon as the ceremony was over. *Mule dung.* He hated being the center of attention, but he would do it for the people. And then he would leave. No one would know, not even Belanor. With new resolution and a real plan, Traian entered the mountain.

Chapter 5

In the next hour, Traian bathed in the frigid waters of
the underground lake by the light of the glowing moonstone
flower he had planted last spring. He changed into his other
set of hunter's trousers and tunic, packed a travel bundle and
took it down to his old burdei, and then he waited patiently
by the cave entrance for Belanor. The sun had already dipped
behind the mountains at his back. Various peaks across the
valley took on a violet and rosy hue.

Traian would miss this view, but nothing would
change his resolve. Not even Belanor. He watched the
magnificent winged horse land on the cliff ledge with the
grace of a swan. Bucking mules, Traian would miss his friend
too.

Ready? Belanor lowered his head so Traian could jump
onto his back.

"Are you planning on flying me to the village square?"

*No, but I will soar over the square and show you where you
need to stand and tell you what to say.*

"Ah." Traian rolled his neck before mounting the horse.

Soon they were in the sky circling the village square high above the trees. Residents bustled about finishing the last of the preparations for the big event. As the heavens darkened, Traian would need to be down there for the opening ceremony.

You will start under the floral arch at the east and move to the feast fire at the center. One of the women will give you the offering tray for you to carry to the fire. You must circle the fire thrice and set the tray at the western base of the blaze. Then you will raise your arms up to the sky facing the flames and say the blessing. Belanor continued with the instructions as they flew around and around.

The more Traian heard, the more he wished to move up his plan of leaving. Traian's stomach twisted into tight knots as he gathered his nerve to meet his doom. It wouldn't take much to muck the complicated ritual.

It's that simple, concluded Belanor. *And don't worry about the blessing, I'll tell you what to say then.*

"Right." Traian glanced at the western orange horizon and to the east where a glowing full moon had emerged. "Better head down there and get this over with."

Worry not, Hunter. I'll watch from here and will guide you.

"Thank you, friend." Traian patted Belanor's neck as they descended to a nearby opening in the forest.

Traian hopped down and sauntered into the village. He resisted the urge to snatch his travel roll and quiver and make a run for the eastern mountain range. Instead, he continued to the village square where he met the councilwoman. She smiled at Traian and wrapped a golden cape over his shoulders, holding it there with a green pin in the shape of a leaf.

Another woman placed a tray filled with the first fruits of summer, cheese, bread, and meat all surrounding a small stone goddess figurine. Most of the village had already gathered around the square. The chatter and laughter quickly died as he stepped under the grand floral arch that had been erected for the festival.

Go. Belanor's command had a gentle but firm tone.

Traian took the first step and paused to lift the tray up to chest level. He continued forward to the fire, circling the dancing flames three times, before placing the tray on the eastern side. He sensed all the eyes boring right through him. *They know I'm a fraud.* He gulped hard and steeled his gaze to the blaze before him. Traian then raised his arms and waited for the words from Belanor.

One by one they came and Traian repeated them out loud with a steady voice. "My beloved townsfolk, summer has come. The first harvest has been collected. The sun warms our earth, bodies, and spirits. We bless the season of growth and celebrate the gifts the earth provides. We bless the earth for its bounty. We bless the sun for its warmth. We bless the moon for lighting the night. We thank the goddess for providing us shelter, food, and the comforts of life. Tonight, let us celebrate this bounty. Let us make merry. Let us dance the Mating Dance. Let us enjoy one another. Let us fill our hearts with love, our bellies with food, our spirits with merriment, and our minds with the joys of our earth. Blessed be."

Silence followed his words. No one moved. The only sound Traian could hear was his own heart pounding in his chest. *Have I failed?* Traian thought and lowered his arms. His answer came with an eruption of applause and cheers. His shoulders drooped as he sighed with relief.

Very good, Hunter. Belanor spoke. *I'm off to do my rounds. Thank you, friend.*

Music started and the people began to dance in circles around the fire. He slowly made his way to the food tables and filled a plate with a sampling of all the delicacies offered. If there was one thing Traian could say about these people... he enjoyed their food. He'd tasted more varieties of vegetables, fruits, cheeses, and meat than any time before. He ate well every day since the moment he'd stepped into this valley—another perk Traian would miss when he left.

Near the periphery of the square, Traian found a stump and sat to watch the merriment while he devoured the feast on his plate. He savored each mouthful, knowing it would be a long time before he would have another meal as such as this. He let the cheese melt in his mouth a while longer and inhaled the aroma of the bread before biting into the loaf.

A new dance began to form throughout the square. Mostly male and female pairs, but he noted several female-female and two male-male pairs. Normally at festivals, pairs only danced for a few moments before switching partners. Tonight, the couples stayed together the entire time he watched. He also noted how their bodies drew closer and closer. Occasionally, a twosome would disappear into one of the many tents around the square. *The mating dance.*

This was midsummer, as perfect a time for fertility as spring. Traian stopped watching and eating after this realization. He took off his cape and left it on the stump.

"Care to dance?" A young maiden appeared before him. "I know I'm not *her*, but I can bring you great pleasure." She rolled her hips at him. Her loose dress dipped down revealing a pair of plump breasts.

"I would be honored, but I'm on duty tonight. Do enjoy yourself though," Traian replied and bowed to the damsel.

"Suit yourself." She tossed her head back and turned to

the dancing crowd.

I need to get out of here. Traian made a quick escape between two tents where groans of passion could be heard in time with the music. He reached the burdei where his meager belongs were stored. The sounds of the festival were muted here. When Traian entered, he had planned to grab his bundle and go, but the shadowed hearth drew his attention.

A strange desire to see one last fire there overwhelmed his wish for a swift departure. From the left of the stone fireplace, he gathered kindling. On instinct, Traian was about to reach into his bundle for the spark stone when he consciously decided to try something he'd never done before.

Traian placed the kindling and logs strategically in the fireplace as he had done countless times. But this time he hovered a hand over the stacked wood and took a deep breath. Just as earlier in the day when he had called on the fire, his palm lit up. Both did. Within a flash, a mighty blaze erupted within the hearth. Traian backed away from the heat.

"This will come in handy." Traian closed both hands, extinguishing the flames.

He sat back watching the fire dance around in a hypnotic manner. This place held many memories that would stick with him for the rest of his life. Each one he would carry no matter where his path led from here. These kind people would live in his heart forever. Traian stopped there. He would not let himself think of Zara or Evelina. Nor Belanor. He loved them too, but he couldn't live like this anymore. *No more secrets.*

Traian stood and picked up the bundle and quiver. He closed his eyes to whisper a short blessing.

"Going somewhere?"

Traian's heart almost stopped beating at the sound of Evelina's soft voice.

Chapter 6

Blasted mule's dung. All the muscles in Traian's face tightened so he wouldn't spit out the string of curses whisking around in his mind like angry hornets. His belly, however, waged a different war. Traian dared not look at Evelina because he sensed his resolve fading with every breath. He concentrated on the fire drawing energy to shield his body and mind from any of her magic.

"Are you going to try to stop me?" Traian asked.

"No." Evelina's answer came without hesitancy.

Traian turned and walked toward the door, but kept his vision aimed on the ground. Evelina stepped aside to give him room. When he tried to pass, her arm came up and barred his exit.

"Answer me one question before you go," Evelina said. "Why are you leaving?"

The uneasy tension inside Traian's belly turned into an angry forest fire. He forced himself to turn and face her. "Must you really ask?" *Don't be tempted by her beautiful face or her mesmerizing eyes. Gods, did she have to wear a red dress? Do.*

Not. Look. Down. His hands tightened into balls.

Evelina kept the steely, emotionless mask on. All the elven folk wore it with such ease. "I kept my promise."

Traian's will to keep calm snapped like a brittle twig. "Oh, bless the goddess, you did." Traian stepped back and waved his arms.

"Why are you angry?" Evelina's brow furrowed — the first hint her cool façade had limits.

"Why am I angry?" Traian scoffed. "Hmm, where do I start?"

"Please tell me," Evelina dropped her arm from the doorway and placed both hands on her hips. "I'd like to hear it all."

"Oh, ha ha." Traian waved a finger at her. "I see your game. You're trying to stop me, and I'm not falling for it."

Evelina stepped forward until she stood toe to toe with him. "I want to know why you are choosing to abandon your people…and us… now, of all times. That is all."

"I'm done." Traian towered over Evelina. "I'm done with the secrets. I'm done with magic. I'm done with being left in the dark while you go frolic with your beloved."

Evelina jerked her head back. "Is this about Padrick?"

"No," Traian answered without thinking, but changed his mind. "Yes. But he's only part of the problem."

"Padrick is the only friend I have in my world, and he saved your life and mine too."

Traian shook his head. "No, that isn't the point. How come I've known you for more than six months, and only this morning you chose to let me know your true identity as the crown princess of Transpatia. The place I didn't know existed until you were poisoned which was three months after you revealed you lived with a dragon?" He drew a breath.

Evelina opened her mouth to say something and then closed it. "Huh." She spun on a heel and started pacing — another elven trait. "My life is complicated. I don't withhold information to be deceitful and most certainly not to hurt you." She paused next to Traian. "Elves are private to a fault."

"I would never have known." Traian shrugged and glared at her.

"Huh." Evelina resumed walking in circles. Her red dress danced around her body accentuating the inviting curves. "You wouldn't understand."

Gods. Traian had to stare at the ceiling to keep from gawking at Evelina's body. "No, and you've never given me a chance. I don't know what you and Zara thought I would do when you brought me here, but I've had enough of these games."

"How can you say that?" Evelina raised her voice,

which surprised Traian. "I taught you how to fight, to channel
the magic within you, and how to protect your mind, of which
you are doing an excellent job right now."

"Yes, but you withhold more than you give." Traian's
answer stopped Evelina in her tracks.

"This morning I told —"

He held a hand up cutting her off. "Information isn't
the only thing you withhold." Traian took a step toward the
doorway. "You tease, but you never give in, and I'm through.
My heart has taken enough." With that, he pushed the
wooden door open and walked out.

Traian inhaled deeply. He'd done it. He'd told Evelina
how he felt. He'd held his ground, and now it was time to
move on. The first step forward seemed shaky, but the next
had more resolve. He ignored the torment in his heart. *Hearts
heal.*

"But I came back," Evelina called behind him, "to you."

This time Traian stopped in his tracks.

"I could have stayed in Transpatia, not for long, but at
least for the festival and night. I could have chosen an elven
mate, but I didn't. I chose you. I came back to you and kept
my word. Blast the elven laws that forbid me to love a human.
I would rather lose my head for giving myself to you than
choose one of the puppets my father has lined up for me."

Oh, why did she have to say these things? Traian anguished. Guilt stung his soul. His mind told Traian this was another ploy to keep him here, but his heart throbbed with the truth of Evelina's words.

"I'm sorry I waited so long. That is my fault," Evelina continued. "I let my own fears rule my heart."

Traian turned halfway to face her. "They'd chop your head off for mating with me?"

Evelina's eyes grew wide as she nodded. "I'm already in trouble for keeping a dragon. It's only a matter of time before they will come here to destroy Zara and then me. If you and I mate, I'm done."

"Oh, so you want a have a little romp with a human before you meet your doom, is that it?" As hard as he tried, Traian couldn't keep his cynical side from speaking up and he hated himself for saying the hurtful words.

"No, I want to stop worrying about laws I no longer should be held accountable for since I've already been ostracized from my world. I want to live life my way." Evelina stepped forward. "And love."

The temperature in Traian's body began to rise. His trousers felt too tight. "But you went back there today."

"A grave mistake on my behalf." Evelina inched closer. "I will tell you everything, I promise, but right now I want to give you what we both have wanted for a long time."

Evelina's words were more like a magic spell to Traian's ears. They trickled through his body like the effects a strong ale. His head jerked to face her. "Stop with all the magic."

She froze mid stride. "I'm not. No magic. This is me speaking my heart."

"You are trying to keep me here."

"Yes, I admit to wanting that, but I would never use my body to convince you to stay. You must remain because you want to." Evelina edged closer. "If you choose to leave, I want you to do so knowing the full truth."

Traian closed his eyes. A war of will and want waged in every corner of his body. Part of him desired to believe every word from Evelina's mouth, to soak them in, and breathe them out. Another vital part of Traian's body certainly wanted more. But the hunter side of him wanted to run as far away from her as from an isolated bear cub. When Evelina moved closer, Traian stepped away but not too far. They circled each other, keeping enough distance to avoid touch. Almost like the mating dance, he'd seen earlier at the festival. He had no expectation of a mating ritual here.

"You are cruel," Traian whispered.

"I don't mean to be." Evelina's voice lowered. "You

have no idea how hard this has been for me."

"I doubt it."

The more the two circled, the closer they got until Traian felt Evelina's warm breath on his neck. He had resisted long enough, but now he couldn't remember why he had fought her in the first place or why he had been angry. The only thing Traian wanted now was to carry Evelina back into the burdei and show her everything he'd wanted to do with her for the last six months.

"You're killing me."

"And you me," she said in a raspy, low voice.

"They'd have to destroy me first before they could ever lay a hand on you." Traian's will snapped, and he gave in. Desire smoldered into a raging fire. He couldn't resist any longer. With one hand, Traian gripped Evelina's waist, and the other swept her up from behind her knees. Evelina wrapped her arms around his neck. Their lips met, and energy crackled at the contact.

Traian carried Evelina into the hut with urgency. If he didn't do this now, he would lose her forever. Inside, he laid Evelina down on his old bed of furs. The travel bundle, quiver, and all other items fell onto the dirt floor. Traian studied the slender beauty lying on his bed and sucked in his breath. He'd dreamt of this moment hundreds of times, and now it was about to come true. Evelina's smooth, pale skin glowed in the light of the fire.

Their lips ignited as they pressed each other's bodies together until they couldn't possibly get closer. Evelina finally pulled away and drew a breath.

"Wait. Before we move forward, I must let you know." Evelina inhaled as Traian caressed her neck. "Listen, this is important."

"I'm—" Traian kissed her shoulder—"listening."

"Elves mate for life."

Traian stopped and raised his head. "Good. Then you'll be stuck with me until I turn into a shriveled old berry and die."

"You don't mind?" Evelina bit down on her lower lip.

"Mind?" Traian caressed the side of her face. "You've had my heart since the day I spotted you in the village square handing out bundles of herbs to the people… the day I arrived."

Evelina's face softened. "You stole my heart that day too. Don't tell Zara I said that."

"Speaking of her, she's been missing since you left."

"Oh, she's fine." Evelina laughed. "She's hunting in the south. I told her to stay away awhile so we could have some privacy. Belanor too."

"Then what are we waiting for?" Those were the last words the lovers spoke as both gave into their passion and their souls sealed together forever.

Epilogue

Traian opened his eyes and stared at the rock wall in front of his desk. He tucked the strong memory into the depths of his mind where he'd hidden it for thousands of years. During the next moment, he felt a presence in his conscience. The sudden intrusion made him stand fast and knock over the chair in the process. Instinctively, his hand readied to retrieve the knife up his sleeve.

But no one was in the room with him. He used his master strigoi ability to listen to each coven member through the network of caves. Nothing stood amiss. Each busied themselves with their duties and while settling into their new home.

Who is there? Traian let his conscience speak.

No answer.

Satra?

No answer. But the presence existed and remained, and Traian couldn't shake it off.

Of course, it wasn't Satra. She never communicated

with him using her mind. Instead, he followed its beacon…
past his coven members, through the tunnels and the steel
door… all the way to the nursery at a hospital in Braşov two
hundred kilometers from the cave.

At half past midnight, Traian entered undetected. He'd
been there before. He made monthly rounds through the
hospitals of the area to check on humans who lay at death's
threshold and needed *comfort* as they passed on. But he'd
never gone into the nursery. The charge nurse fed a bottle to
the baby in her arms while talking on the phone. Tonight, five
infants occupied the twelve cradles. Each newborn's aura
sparkled in bright pink light, except for the fifth.

Her aura was pitch black, yet her pale face appeared as
that of an angel. She was completely at peace, almost as if she
knew Traian had come for her and was okay with it. He felt an
overpowering need to caress her cheek. The child was warm
with fever. She opened her eyes and looked right at him. In
the dim light, Traian knew she could not possibly see him
because her eyesight had not developed yet. He shivered as
her tiny green eyes pierced deep into his soulless body. She
was the presence he'd sensed, the one who had brought him
to this place.

Save me. Her young voice rang in his head.

Traian removed his hand and stepped back with

lightning speed. The child's eyes followed his movement and continued staring. Traian ventured a step back as the newborn continued to gaze at him, opening her mouth into a big yawn. *How do I save her?* Traian toiled with the thought when he mindlessly touched her warm forehead.

Fragile, innocent, and so sweet. Her small eyelids fluttered as if she heard his inner thoughts. *Evelina?* He opened his mind to her.

What a funny name. She yawned again. *Please save me.*

Traian bit into his wrist and squeezed two drops of blood into the infant's open mouth. The effect was instant; tiny, pink patches appeared within her black aura. She blinked once slowly and then closed her eyes.

Thank you, she said as her little mind drifted into the land of nod. Her presence disappeared from Traian's mind.

He leaned over the cradle and kissed her cheek before slipping out of the room unnoticed. Thousands of thoughts raced through his mind, but he couldn't disregard one. *Could she be Evelina?*

To be continued…

Acknowledgments

Thank you so much for reading the Legends of Carpatia story collection. Your review is much appreciated and helps others discover this series.

It takes a village to write and publish a book. I want to thank my village which includes Nicole Asmus, Kathy Lapeyre and Sara Lunsford for editing and teaching me to write better, Dr. Scott Burns, Eric Hudson for proofreading, Victoria Cooper for the gorgeous covers, Gigi and Myleeta for watching my girl so I can write and edit, My Wise Women goddesses, my beta-readers and reviewers (a thousand thank you's), and glorious readers who took a chance on this book. I am forever grateful to my family and friends who support me every day.

The Silver Cross (The Silver Series) coming summer of 2018.

About the Author

Melania Tolan lives in the Pacific Northwest with her husband, daughter, and two geriatric felines. When she's not writing or working at day job, you can find her exploring the outdoors, binge-watching sci-fi shows on *Netflix*, or sampling the local cider production.

www.ingramcontent.com/pod-product-compliance
Lightning Source LLC
Chambersburg PA
CBHW021056130626
46552CB00005B/2122